MALUM DISCORDIAE

A HAUNTED NEW ORLEANS NOVEL

RAYVN SALVADOR

Malum Discordiae

A Haunted New Orleans Novel

By Rayvn Salvador

MALUM DISCORDIAE

A HAUNTED NEW ORLEANS NOVEL

RAYVN SALVADOR

Cover Design: Kari March Designs

Editing: Red Head Editing

Published by: Lady Boss Press, Inc.

For all those who believe . . . in whatever you believe. Thank you for being brave enough to do so.

PROLOGUE

October 15.

Archived journal entry of reporter Sam Dean -
The Bayou Beat

*F*ULL MOONS AND ECLIPSES BRING INTERESTING ENERGIES THAT CORRELATE WITH UNUSUAL ACTIVITY, THOUGH NONE SO MUCH AS THIS MONTH'S HARVEST MOON.

At 4:54 a.m. on Thursday, Oct. 8th, dispatch sent the New Orleans police department to an antebellum mansion in the Garden District, following a call from a disgruntled neighbor, complaining of a disturbance starting at approximately three o'clock.

When the officers arrived on the scene, it was to a tableau of murder and mayhem. Several people were dead, the back portion of the home was

PARTIALLY IN FLAMES, AND THE LEVEL OF DESTRUCTION WAS BEYOND COMPREHENSION.

WITNESSES STATE THAT RUMORS HAD RUN RAMPANT OVER THE YEARS THAT A DARK COVEN OF *"DEVIL-WORSHIP-PING"* WITCHES CALLED THE DOMICILE HOME—ONE DUBBING THEMSELVES THE *MOON CALL* COVEN. IN THE MIDST OF THE SO-CALLED SATANIC PANIC, HOWEVER, ONE CANNOT PUT MUCH STOCK IN SUCH RUMBLINGS WITHOUT PLENTY OF PROOF. STILL, SOME OF THE THINGS WE WERE ABLE TO CAPTURE ON FILM LEAD TO SPECULATION.

ALTARS, THRONES, ANTI-CHRISTIAN ART, AND SCULP-TURES WERE SEEN THROUGHOUT THE HOUSE, AND THE RESIDENCE SEEMED TO BE OUTFITTED SOMEWHAT LIKE A COMMUNE, WITH MULTIPLE UNRELATED PERSONS LIVING UNDER THE SAME ROOF—SOMETIMES THREE OR MORE TO A BEDROOM.

THE POLICE HAVE NOT YET RELEASED THE NUMBER OF CASUALTIES, THE IDENTITIES OF THE DECEASED, THEIR CAUSES OF DEATH, NOR ANY PERSONS OF INTEREST, BUT OUR SOURCES HAVE CONFIRMED THAT A PRIEST WAS AT THE CENTER OF THE EVENTS. TO WHAT DEGREE AND IN WHAT CAPACITY, I HAVE NOT YET ASCERTAINED, NOR HAVE I ROOTED OUT HIS IDENTITY, BUT *THE BEAT*'S INVESTIGA-TORS ARE HARD AT WORK, AND I'M EXCITED TO WRITE THIS STORY.

~S.D.

CHAPTER 1

~Schuyler~

I pulled up to the Lamour Mansion and parked on the street, taking in the grand estate's sprawling architecture and antebellum charm. The lantern-topped stone pillars holding the ornate gate, and the wrought iron fence with its peacock-feather-motif spearheads beckoned like a siren's call. I'd always been a sucker for beautiful buildings, and New Orleans had some of the best. There was nothing like deep-South charisma in my mind, and Louisiana offered it in spades from the vast plantations to the raised-center-hall cottages to the double-gallery mansions. Even the shotgun houses held a special brand of appeal.

Looking across the street, I saw Paxton's vintage,

cherry-red F-Series pickup near the curb, the magnet for his soup kitchen affixed to the driver's side door. The classic was in mint condition, and I knew he hated parking it on the busy side of the street.

Nice of him to leave me the mansion's curbside parking spot, though.

During our video call this morning, Deveraux Glapion, creator and host of the paranormal reality show I worked for—*Haunted New Orleans*—renowned Vodou Houngan, and descendant of none other than Marie Laveau, had asked Paxton and me to do a preliminary check of our next property as they continued their research on Arborwood, the show's current location. Things weren't quite going according to plan at the plantation house, but I was confident that the team could get things back on track and finish in time to get to this beaūty. Assuming no more murders waylaid us, of course. The terror that the RƎDRΩM killer was wreaking on the city needed to stop. After working for the Louisiana State Police crime lab for years, I'd been called in as a consultant a couple of years ago to work one of the murders. It was something I'd never forget. Especially since it had been the death of a relative of someone I knew. The feelings I'd experienced trying to get to the bottom of that case— with no results—were something that haunted me to this day. Just the thought of it quickened my pulse and shortened my breath. And I knew it still plagued the others involved, as well.

I glanced back up at the estate's massive twenty-thousand-square-foot expanse and wondered where we'd even start. Despite the daunting task in front of us, I couldn't deny my excitement. For some reason, this house had always called to me. I didn't know if it was the building itself or the energy of it.

Yes, energy. While I didn't really believe in the supernatural—I was a scientist and dealt in facts and absolutes—I *did* believe in harmonious energy forces. Chalk it up to my upbringing and my parents' beliefs. However, with that said, in all my years working with Dev and the cast and crew of *Haunted New Orleans*, I couldn't deny that I had seen and experienced things that were odd and intriguing. Sometimes, a little mind-blowing. At the end of the day, I firmly believed there was science behind it somewhere. Still, the evidence to argue otherwise was compelling. Enough to convert me? Hell, no! But . . . I'd keep an open mind. Sort of. I'd still proudly wear my SKEPTIC sash and crown while giving a nod—albeit tiny—to the things I'd seen and experienced over time, and what the team could do.

As for Paxton . . . the things *he* believed in were most definitely supernatural to me. I was firmly in the there-are-no-gods corner, and I was pretty sure that nobody could convince me otherwise. I could some-times get on board with some of Lark's and Dev's beliefs since they paid homage to multiple supposed deities and worked with the energy of the Universe, but putting all your eggs in one basket for a single supreme being that lorded over—pun intended—all of us wasn't something I could wrap my head around.

To each their own, of course. Life took all kinds, after all. But the stalwart belief that everything you did on Earth was being weighed on some grand, cosmic scale and presided over by a single judge who would determine whether you were happy after death or not wasn't something I could entertain. At least, not yet. Put the evidence in front of me, and I'd be happy to do the experiments and re-evaluate. But not until. Besides, death was death.

Yes, I worked for a paranormal reality show, and my paychecks came from investigating the presumed existence of ghosts and other supernatural entities, but while I had seen some things that made me go "hmm," it was my job to debunk, disprove, and explain a lot of the stuff that the team discovered during an investigation. I didn't completely *dis*believe the things that Dev and the others dredged up—I had seen some of it with my own eyes—I just simply believed there was a logical explanation for it all. Somewhere. We just hadn't found it yet or figured out *how* to explain it. My years with the crime lab for the LSP had given me some unique experience into things that looked one way and were, in reality, another.

It brought me great pleasure to work with Lennie and Van, our two engineers—and even Harper, our psychologist—to disprove things the homeowners and other witnesses reported. Or rather prove that it was copper pipes, grounded house electricity, or strange acoustics and nothing woo-woo. That the black mold, carbon monoxide, contaminated groundwater, or lead in the paint caused hallucinations, and that there was nothing to fear but the cost of your home remodeling bill. We even had another non-believer in the mix right now with Hanlen, Arborwood's owner and Dev's new girlfriend. As she put it, she didn't believe in any of the hullabaloo either. *Skeptics unite!*

Pulling myself out of my thoughts and grabbing the file of information we'd all been given, I locked the car and started towards the sidewalk that ran along the front of the property. Passing under the large crepe myrtle that arched over the walk, I took in the shock of bright pink blooms standing out like a highlighter streak against today's crystal-clear, blue sky. For the thousandth time, I lamented that my stick-straight, jet-black hair didn't bleach well enough to take fun fashion colors. I proudly let my freak flag fly with my white and black, double-winged eyeliner and Harajuku girl style, although often downplayed for public consumption to my favorite crazy boots, and pithy—sometimes, insulting—novelty T-shirts. But my hair was forever boring—at least, to me. Unless I clipped in an extension, which I did occasionally.

I readjusted my forensics kit in my left hand and pushed open the gate, the creak of its hinges letting me know that it had been here for some time. From what I'd read in our preliminary report, the Lamour Mansion had been built in 1852 by a cotton farmer named Aristide Lamour and had been passed down through the generations until the family died out. After that, it became a boarding school for a time before a starlet and her artist husband purchased it in the 1920s. I wasn't sure what'd happened after that, but there were a lot of rumors. I was confident the team would get to the bottom of it, and I couldn't deny that I was excited to find out more.

Since Pax was already here, I pocketed the key that Dev had given to me and headed up the steps of the mansion's wide, wrap-around porch. A large swing hung to my left, and the right had an arrangement of inviting-looking outdoor furniture. Topiaries flanked the large door with its new stained-glass window. I wondered when that had been installed. It was stunning. I was glad the estate had been kept up and apparently cleaned regularly—at least outside of the construction mess—despite the fact that nobody had actually called it home for a very long time.

I rapped with a single knuckle on the door and pushed it wide, revealing a breathtaking interior. The light streaming in from the floor-to-ceiling windows made the hardwood floors gleam and hit the curved arches and Corinthian fluted cypress columns that served as picturesque frames for the receiving room to my left, the parlor to my right, and the dual sweeping staircases that met at a grand shared landing straight ahead.

I looked up to see the massive brass-and-crystal-teardrop chandelier swaying gently in a breeze I couldn't feel. Maybe Paxton was on the second floor. Since we were the only ones here, I decided to forgo manners and called out for him.

"Honey, I'm ho-o-o-me. Pax, you around?" My words echoed in the open space, bouncing off the vaulted ceilings. I wondered if he'd even answer me. Most everyone called him *Padre*—even I did in my head sometimes—but to his face, I couldn't do it for some reason. I wondered if it was my subconscious's way of keeping the fact that he used to be a priest out of my mind.

I was sure that he had heard me, even on the second level if that were, indeed, where he was. But just in case he was somewhere he *wouldn't* hear, I decided to take a quick look around the ground floor instead of yelling again. As I walked, my footsteps echoing all around the space, I grabbed my pen out of my bun and made a note on my paperwork to do some baseline readings of the sound transference in the room and get Van to measure directionality. That way, if we heard any disembodied voices, footsteps, or banging, or got any electronic voice phenomena on the recorders during the investigation, we could tag them and check the cameras to be sure it wasn't just someone in another part of the house.

I stopped in the enormous kitchen with its stunning cabinetry and vintage butcher block island in the center of the room and looked through to the cook's kitchen, butler's pantry, and the arch of the dining room beyond, listening for footsteps. Nothing yet. I set my stuff on the surface of a credenza next to a curio cabinet full of what looked to be priceless china and made some notes on the map that we had all been given.

Ready to check the other side of the house before heading upstairs, I straightened and turned, taking my first step, only to run nose-first into a rock-hard wall. Or a chest, rather. A very sculpted set of pecs that smelled of Hugo Boss. Immediately noticing the heat seeping into my arms from the callused hands now gripping me, I looked up into eyes the color of a winter morning—blue and crisp and breath-stealing.

Paxton Chase was a very handsome man. At least a decade my senior, he had that distinguished-gentleman thing going for him, tempered by the fact that he was a no-fuss kind of guy. He preferred flannels to suit coats. His pickup to Town Cars. And would likely laugh in your face if you offered him a glass of wine. But then there was the whole used-to-be-a-priest thing. Still, the man was yummy—not that I'd ever tell him that.

"Are you okay?" he asked, his deep drawl hitting me in the solar plexus.

I straightened and tugged away, tucking a stray piece of hair behind my ear and shoving my pen back in my bun. "Yeah, I'm fine. Sorry. I didn't hear you come in. Which is strange, because this place echoes worse than that underground fuel depot in Scotland that holds the latest world record."

Pax smiled. "You are a font of useless information. Did anyone ever tell you that?"

I shrugged. "Once or twice. And who says it's

useless?" I flashed him a smile. "Okay, so, what's the four-one-one? How long have you been here?"

He looked around the place. "Not long. Maybe forty-five minutes or so. Just did a quick sweep to familiarize myself and get a feel. When did you get here?"

I checked my watch. "Less than ten minutes ago. I took in the outside for a bit—the front, anyway—and just came in. Didn't make it any farther than the kitchen. Did Dev give you any direction for what exactly he wanted us to do or look for today?"

Pax ran a hand along the scruff on his jaw and shook his head. "Nah, not really. Just said he wanted a team in here to do a walk-through, make some notes on the map like you were doing, and scope out some good places for equipment. He did say that if we wanted to do a daytime EVP session, maybe do a Handycam tour, he'd like that. Might give the super twins some baseline readings for noise distortion, and R2, James, and Aaron some ideas for equipment needs and whatnot."

He got an odd look, and I was almost afraid of what he was going to say next. He took a deep breath, and I couldn't help but redistribute my weight and cross my arms. "Just spit it out. Clearly, you have something you need to say but don't want to," I said.

He sighed. "There's an exposed, walled-off area towards the back of the house. Near the bit where the damage occurred thirty-odd years ago. The contractors and builders were just getting going back there, and that's where Roch told us his guys have been having the most issues."

Roch Lasear was the general contractor for the latest crew working on the mansion for the current owners. He was the one who'd reached out to *Haunted New Orleans* about the investigation since, according to him, the stuff that had been happening lately had ramped up a lot, and he was running out of crewmembers willing to stay and finish the job.

"Yeah, and?" I prompted.

He rubbed his middle and ring fingers against his forehead. "You're the smallest in the crew. Dev wants you to get up into the crawl space and take a look around."

"Lark's not much bigger than me."

"Yeah, but Birdie doesn't have your scientific knowledge. She doesn't know to look for things that could be contributing to what's going on in the house—the stuff that's scaring the workers. She'd be tuned into the spiritual side of things. Right now, we need the basics. Scientific data. And you're our best bet."

I looked down at my NOT A ZOMBIE, BUT I FEEL LIKE ONE T-shirt, mesh hoodie, and my favorite distressed black jeans and blew out a breath.

"I've got a jumpsuit for you in the other room. The fashion will be fine, princess."

I knew he was teasing me, but my hackles still rose. "Like you care, Mr. Brawny."

He plucked the corner of his plaid shirt. "Ouch."

"Just giving you shit, *Father*. All right, let's get this

over with. It's a good thing I'm not claustrophobic." I set off to where I thought the area in question was, Pax following closely. As we got deeper into the house, I started to feel . . . off. I'd have to do some environmental readings before we left today to see if anything in the air could be causing that. Just as I was thinking about the equipment I'd need, Pax interrupted my thoughts.

"It's not nice in here."

I looked at him. "What do you mean? This part's not as bad as I assume the area that got messed up all those years ago is. Kind of beautiful, actually. Not as nice as the front, of course, but still nice."

"I meant energetically. Spiritually. It's just . . . I dunno. Heavy. Oppressive. Feels . . . wrong. It's weird."

"Ahh. I was just thinking the same, and I don't usually get feelings like that. I wonder if the fire damage and the subsequent aging got some nasty shit growing in the walls. I'll get some samples and readings before we head out."

Pax moved ahead of me to open a door, and I couldn't stop my gaze from dropping to his very fine ass. Sue me. He may not care about fashion, but he could fill out a pair of jeans with the best of 'em. Most of the guys on the cast and crew could. It was a smorgasbord of man candy delight. Probably not the most politically correct thing to think, but I couldn't help myself. And it was true. And that was before you factored in the beauty of the women. Not to mention, we had something for everyone from sports junkies to intellectuals; angelic redheads to feisty brunettes; the sensitive, quiet ones, to outspoken nonbelievers; millennials to Gen-Xers. There was more than one reason the show did so well for the network. Yes, we were professionals, but we had become actors, too. And as the agent I'd never wanted but had been forced to get constantly told me, *"Your look and your personality have now become your brand, Sky. Own it, and you'll own the audience."*

As we rounded the corner into the area of the home where the most damage had occurred and the construction was in full effect, the hairs on my arms rose. Something was definitely going on here. "Did you by any chance take any electromagnetic field readings while you were in here earlier?" I asked.

"I did. The K2 had the EMF toggling between zero-point-one and zero-point-two to one-point-nine. And it wasn't consistent. Not where you could definitively say there was some sort of environmental cause. We'll need to look into it more." He peered at me, his brow rising. "You felt it, too, then?"

"Yeah, strange. Kind of like static. But as always with high electromagnetic frequencies, that feeling of being watched, too."

"Exactly. And as we know, high EMF can go one way or the other. Either it acts as a beacon and battery and leads to more legitimate paranormal experiences, or it *is* the experience, causing the person to feel however they are." He walked around the sawhorses and other construction equipment and debris lying around to the far corner and pointed up. The wall had a jagged gap between concrete and drywall and ceiling, beyond which lay a yawning void of darkness.

"I take it that's the place?" I asked. "Not a crawl space if it's off the ground, Pax."

"Fair point. I just didn't know what else to call it. But, yes, that's the place." He leaned over and picked up a white jumpsuit, goggles, a headlamp, and a mask and handed them to me. "Your costume for the day."

I rolled my eyes. "Ah, just what I always wanted. Who's the designer? Odd? Toga? Ponti?"

"All I just heard was '*blah, blah, blah.*'"

I laughed. I couldn't help it. I double-tapped him on the cheek with the lengths of my fingers. "It's okay, *Papi.* I know it's hard for that old brain to compute such modern concepts, especially when it comes to fashion." I set the gear on a little table nearby and unzipped the jumpsuit, stepping into it. When I looked up, Pax had an odd look on his face and the set of his shoulders was stiff.

"What?" I asked.

He squinted, causing his brow to wrinkle. "Why do you do that?" he asked.

I frowned. "Do what?"

"Constantly poke fun. You rarely call me *Padre* like the rest of the team, but you never seem to miss a chance to call me something similar that I know you don't mean in a nice way."

I furrowed my brow and shook my head. "I didn't mean anything by it, honest."

"Whatever," he said and turned away to grab a step stool.

Someone's touchy. But I had to wonder . . . *did* I do that? I thought about it for a second. Yeah, I did. Huh. I'd have to watch myself. I hadn't realized it bothered him so much.

When I secured the hood and donned the mask, goggles, and headlamp, I turned around and found Pax staring at me.

"Don't you dare laugh. You laugh, and I will punch you in the 'nads. Seriously."

"What? I didn't say anything."

"Your face says it all, mister." I pointed and circled my finger in the direction of said face. "Now, how are we doing this?"

He indicated the stool. "Hop on up. I'll give you a boost, and you can crawl on in. Then I'll hand you the bag of equipment. It doesn't look to be so bad once you're in there. It's the getting in that's tight. Once you clear that, you should have a bit of room to maneuver and even stand if you want. But we have absolutely no idea what's up there or when in the last one hundred and sixty-odd years it was put there. This area could be original, or it could be something they modified— which would be my guess if I had to wager. We just aren't sure yet. So, I guess what I'm saying is . . . be careful."

"Always," I said and got up onto the stool, hopping up to brace myself on the ledge of the opening. "It would have been nice if someone had left the ladder I

16

assume was used to access this before they walled it off. Okay, boost me."

Pax's hands went to the backs of my thighs and the curve of my butt, and I couldn't help but suck in a breath. *I did mention that he's hot, right?* Once I had some leverage, I hoisted myself over the ledge and swung my legs into the dark space with the rest of me, clicking on my headlamp, only to come face-to-face with a body part.

A freaking hand.

I let loose a scream that could probably rouse the dead.

CHAPTER 2

~Paxton~

Schuyler's startled shriek froze the blood in my veins.

"Sky! What's wrong? Are you okay?" I yelled, scrambling up onto the stool to try and see inside the niche.

"Jesus fucking Christ. I mean . . . um . . . cheese and fluffy rice. Yeah, I'm fine. But holy sea of shit."

That made me laugh, but I had to give her credit for creativity—and for trying. Sort of. I laughed harder but then got serious. She was clearly okay, but I still didn't know what was wrong. "You're killin' me here. What's up?" I called.

"There are freaking mannequin parts up here, Pax. Creepy-ass, life-sized doll pieces. Bodies, I can do.

Soul-stealing, plastic wannabe humans? Nope. Nuh-uh." I heard her shuffling around a bit.

"When I flicked on my headlamp there was a frickin' hand in my face. A *hand*. Scared the ever-lovin' hell out of me." She blew out an audible breath that I heard even from where I stood now down below, and it made me grin. "Get me a bigger flashlight, would ya? I need to take a peek around."

I smiled wider and then stepped up onto the stool so I could reach in farther and hand her the LED flashlight from the pack. Schuyler Liu, fearless forensics expert, lover of horror and disbeliever of anything supernatural was afraid of . . . dummies?

"What do you see?" I asked.

I heard her shuffling around up there some more. "You were right. It's way bigger up here than I expected. I think it was maybe a storage area at one point. Perhaps even a loft of some kind before that, though this is a really strange place for one given the layout of the house. An indoor balcony maybe? Who knows? I see some old Christmas decorations, some dress forms, a storage chest or two. A bunch of antiquey-looking things. And lots and lots of dirt. More than I would think there would or should be. Weirdly, it almost looks like they got fed up and just closed it off completely—with everything inside. Strange, but I've seen stranger. And, let's be real, people can be lazy."

She wasn't wrong. Still, it *was* weird. Why would they have turned a loft or indoor balcony into a storage space and then left everything after trying to fill it in with dirt for some unknown reason—if that's what they did—before sealing it off like the room never existed? Sounded like a crime drama. I guess we'd find out. Hopefully, Burke—our new historian—and Harper could dig up some more in-depth information on the history of the house and the previous owners. For now, Sky and I could get some baseline readings and then finish up here. We needed to check in with the team and see how things went at Arborwood today.

"You ready for the gear? And do you want your kit?"

"Uh . . . yeah. Hold on a sec. I just want to check this closest chest really quick and then I'll crawl back over to grab it from you." I heard her moving again and hoped there weren't any critters up there she'd need to worry about. I didn't think there was access from the outside, but you never knew. And snakes loved places like attics.

"Oh . . . oh, wow," came Sky's voice from above.

"What?" I called.

"There's . . . I'm not entirely sure, but given all the cases we've worked, there are what appear to be hex bags in this chest. At least they look like those I've seen Dev and Birdie identify. Locks of hair. Old jewelry. What appears to be . . . I dunno. Chicken bones, maybe? Everything has a brown glaze. I'd be shocked if it's not blood. We're going to have to take this stuff and have it analyzed. And Dev and Lark are definitely going to want to take a peek. But I'm not touching this shit. At least not more than I already have. I may not believe in it, but I'm not tempting fate regardless. I've seen too many movies."

I chuffed a laugh. "After this many years, it's likely inert if there *is* anything going on with it. But, yeah, don't poke the bear. We'll get Dev or Birdie to negate anything that might be on there before we mess with it more. Is it close enough to the opening for them to access?"

"It's pretty close, but Lark will be able to get up here. And I know she can work her mumbo jumbo just in case. Okay, hand me the bag, the kit, and a camera. I'm going to capture what I can."

I did as she requested and then took a seat on one of the sawhorses, waiting and listening in case she needed me. When I saw a delicate hand poke through the opening, I jumped up and rushed over, taking the bag she held out. Once I had everything out of the crawl space, I waited for her to pull herself closer.

She looked down and took off her mask and goggles. "So, um, how the hell am I supposed to get out of here?" she asked with a quirk of her lip.

"I'm gonna have to help. Hold out your arms, and I'll pull you out partway."

She did as I said, and I stepped up onto the stool, grabbed her under the pits, and pulled her forward until just her pelvis rested on the ledge before stepping down. "Okay, you're going to have to kind of balance yourself and hang on while I pull you the rest of the way out," I said. "Don't worry, I've got you."

"Drop me," she said, "and I will put Nair in your shampoo on our next overnight."

"Vicious little thing, aren't you?" I quirked a smile.

She wrapped her arms around my neck, and I tugged, tensing as her body came into contact with mine, inch by inch. Even through the layers, I felt her curves, and it made my breath hitch. From the moment Dev had introduced Sky to the team four years ago, she had made appearances in my dreams. With those soulful, dark eyes, glossy hair, and her petite yet strong body that she wrapped in the most ridiculous things most days, she was a constant source of intrigue. But she was my coworker. And she was at least ten years younger than me.

I didn't know how old she was, exactly, but I knew she couldn't be older than thirty-five. So, at my forty-five, while it wasn't taboo, it was still a hurdle. Not to mention, I honestly wasn't sure if she even *liked* me. With Sky, sometimes you just couldn't tell. We were workplace friends, sure. But beyond that . . .?

I looked down at her and saw her lips parted a bit. Huh. Seemed she wasn't entirely unaffected by our close proximity either. Being a gentleman, after I made sure she was steady, I let her go and took a step back, grabbing the headlamp from her as I did.

She lowered the hood and unzipped the jumpsuit, stepping out of it and then tucking some stray hair behind an ear.

Her eyes widened, and a look of horror crossed her face. "No. Nonononononono," she suddenly screamed and started doing some sort of crazy dance, jumping around and swatting at herself, twisting her body in unimaginable ways. "Oh, *hell* no." She shucked the mesh hoodie she wore, still flailing as if she were on fire, and then ripped her T-shirt over her head, swatting at herself with the material, leaving her in only a black sports bra and jeans, her muscles bunching interestingly.

My brain just . . . stopped. The creamy swells of her breasts peeked above the scoop of the cotton and her waistband rode low, showing defined obliques and delineated hips. A bright pink jewel sparkled from the dip of her navel. But the most breathtaking reveal was the tattoo on her side. From what I could see of it, it ran from under her arm to below the waistband of her pants and was a stunning piece of art. An apple tree, full of bright red orbs, backlit by some mystical light source. One shiny fruit lay at the base of the tree with a bite missing. It was the Tree of Knowledge—or at least it looked like it—and I couldn't be more stunned.

Shaking myself out of my thoughts and ogling, I realized that she had started to calm. At least, a bit.

"So . . ." I said, "care to share with the class?"

"Fucking spider. I *hate* spiders. Loathe them. All those creepy eyes and legs and . . . fur. Hair. Whatever the hell it is. They are disgusting little creatures." She looked at me then, shaking out her T-shirt before pulling it back over her head. "Maybe you should ask your god why he created them. I mean, what's up with that? 'Cause . . . ew."

I couldn't help it. I busted out in a deep belly laugh. "You're adorable."

She cocked her head. "I know." And then she winked.

After she'd redonned her mesh hoodie, she grabbed her stuff and looked at me. "Where to next?" she asked.

"We should probably go and check out the upstairs," is what I said. What I *really* wanted to ask her about was that tattoo. For an atheist, it seemed an odd choice. Especially given that across most cultures, an apple was always a symbol of temptation and sin. As beautiful as the art was, I sensed there was a deeper meaning there. I wondered if she'd ever tell me.

Once we'd completed what we needed to do at the mansion and had everything recorded both on paper and digitally, we packed everything up and headed out front. The sun was just starting to set. It had been a long day, but it had flown. I helped Sky get all her stuff into her car and then took her in. She looked more tired than usual, and I could see dark circles starting to peek through the makeup on her face.

"Hey, you okay?" I asked.

She stretched. "Yeah, why?"

"You just . . . look kinda tired."

"Ah, such a flatterer." She shook her head. "It was a long day, Pax. I was in a crazy, tight, walled-off room with doll parts of doom and spiders that likely wanted to eat my face, and the EMF in that place made me twitchy the entire time."

"Wait, you felt it all over the estate?" Interesting. I'd

felt that classic uneasy feeling in a couple of places, but not all over the mansion.

"For the most part, yeah. As beautiful as this place is, it kinda gives me the willies. Dev would say bad juju. I just say bad wiring or some weird energy vortex."

"It's funny you should say that. Dev said that he set up a meeting with the local alternative archaeological society to discuss possible ley lines or vortices under the property."

She nodded. "Huh. Good call. You never know." Slamming the trunk, she turned to me more fully. "Well, I suppose I'd better get home. I'm starving. See you tomorrow?"

I reached out without thought and repositioned the pen in her bun, my thumb grazing her cheek as I did. "Drive safely, Sky."

I turned and headed to my truck, wondering how she could get me so twisted up so easily.

Temptation and sin, indeed.

CHAPTER 3

~Schuyler~

J woke, the sun blazing through the window and nailing me in the face like a spotlight. Even with my eyes still closed, I winced. My head had been killing me lately, and I couldn't seem to get the headaches to let up. I probably shouldn't have been surprised. A whole hell of a lot had been going on these last weeks since Pax and I had paid our first visit to the Lamour Mansion, and things wrapped up at Arborwood, and we had been going nearly nonstop before that, bouncing from one location to the next.

I'd held someone at gunpoint at the plantation—someone I knew and actually liked!—after they'd taken someone else I knew hostage, prepared to sacrifice them to their quote-unquote *darkness*, thus revealing that they were the sadistic serial murderer terrorizing the city. The same asshole who'd left no trace for me years ago as I tried to help the police find a woman's killer. I *still* couldn't completely wrap my head around it. I couldn't wrap my head around *a lot* lately.

I'd seen things I couldn't compartmentalize, too; stuff that shook the very fabric of what I believed—or thought I *didn't* believe. And I hadn't had time to process things and put them into their neat little boxes like I usually did, so everything was just sort of floating around out there with a lot of question marks.

We'd also lost another *Haunted New Orleans* member, and the whole dynamic of the team had changed with that, the realization that we had been working with a killer, and the introduction of Hanlen. While I was happy to have her—her private investigative skills alone would be super useful for us—and I really enjoyed her as a person, it'd been a crazy ride.

We'd had to put off any additional investigation on the Lamour Mansion for a while because of everything that'd happened at Arborwood. Thankfully, the network was being really understanding. Again.

Pax and I had been out a couple of times over the weeks with Aaron and James, our new tech grip, Turner, and Birdie to do some one-off things that we needed to do anyway—things we *could* do because the construction crew had halted all their work—but nothing official had happened since Pax and I first went to take a peek around and dig through the weird hidey hole or loft/balcony/catchall space.

That would change later.

Today was our first pre-official-shoot investigation with nearly the entire team. The day we got all our glamour shots and did our walk-throughs and initial readings on camera and started poking around for real. That way, we could take anything we found and try to debunk the findings as much as possible before discovering what things actually had a legitimate paranormal angle to explore—i.e., anything we couldn't immediately explain away. We would bookmark those for the official seventy-two-hour investigation and additional research into the history of the house.

Now that my eyes had been metaphorically opened a bit more to the whole unexplained part of what we did—though I still remained very skeptical—I was kind of excited to see what this investigation turned up, and what I could experiment on to debunk. It was almost like joining the team all over again. The excitement was back. I firmly believed in science, but my need for . . . *more* had initially led me to quitting my CSI job and accepting the position that Dev offered me in the first place. I still did some forensics work as a consultant to buy new shoes and support my collectibles habit, but I was happy to be working in a job where I could flex my muscles and still expand my mind.

Realizing I'd been lazy for too long, I finally got up and did a full-body stretch, noticing that I still felt like crap—achy and stiff and just generally shitty. It'd been too many weeks of this. I should probably get into the doctor. Maybe my iron was low or something. I'd just been feeling super drained and lethargic and not myself. Even my moods had been wonky, but I chalked that up to stress and the fact that I couldn't get a good night's sleep if my life depended on it these days—the dreams I'd been having lately were not letting me get any shut-eye.

After the world's fastest shower and some quick makeup so I didn't look like the walking dead, I twisted my hair into a bun and threw on my T-shirt that declared the year as NO GOOD, VERY BAD, WOULD NOT RECOMMEND with a one-star rating, tucked my jeans into my favorite white lug-soled boots that laced like a corset with black ribbons, and grabbed my butter-soft leather jacket on the way out the door—it always looked good on camera.

Just as I was about to unlock the car, my cell buzzed. I pulled it out of my back pocket and checked the display.

Paxton.

"Yo. What's up?" I unlocked the car and threw my kit and bag into the back.

"Good morning to you, too," Pax drawled. "I was just picking up some java. Wondered if you wanted anything."

"Where?" I asked, digging my favorite pen out of my bag's pocket to shove into my bun since I knew I'd need it.

"Café Du Monde."

"Oh, hell yes. Snag me an iced café au lait and an order of beignets."

"You got it. Maybe I should grab some empty calo- ries and fuel for the rest of the gang, too. Are you heading out soon?" I heard a vehicle door slam over the line and assumed that he'd parked.

"Just throwing stuff in the car now," I said and then got behind the wheel. "Did you talk to Dev at all this morning?"

The murmur of voices came through the phone, and I knew he was getting into line. No matter the time of day, Café Du Monde was always busy, but it was worth the wait and more.

"No," he answered. "But I did talk to Birdie for a bit. She wanted me to bring some things so she could do what she needed to do with the chest you found in the crawl space—or whatever it is."

I'd almost forgotten about that. All that hair and jewelry and . . . I shrugged off a shiver. "What kind of stuff?" I asked, wondering why I cared.

"Holy water, a small crucifix, and a Saint Michael medallion. She mentioned bringing some Florida water and Himalayan salt from her stash, as well as some charged jasper chips, and said she asked Dev to bring a gris-gris bag and some other items from his armory. I think she wants to throw everything we have at this thing. Just in case, you know? Especially after she walked the place and felt what she did."

I nodded, even though he couldn't see me. Larken was labeled a *very gifted psychic* and *practicing witch*— things that I couldn't entirely wrap my head around but accepted as fact, nonetheless. Even I had to admit that she was good at her job, and there seemed to be more to reality than what the average person could perceive. When she visited the mansion with us after the events at Arborwood, she'd told both Pax and me that she believed we might be dealing with some dark forces. Said she'd felt an overwhelming sense of sorrow, and the heavy weight of oppression—and that was only her first impressions without any digging.

"I suppose that makes sense," I said. "It was weird. And, even energetically, we don't need anything messing with the investigation. Besides, given what Roch has told us so far about the shit that his guys were seeing and experiencing, we should probably have that stuff on hand anyhow. Along with things to combat any environmental causes."

"Exactly," he agreed. "All right. I'm up next. See you in a few."

"Okay. Later. Thanks for breakfast."

"Anytime."

He disconnected, and I tossed my phone in the cupholder before popping on my sunglasses, starting the car, and finding my favorite classic alternative station. The day was another gorgeous one. The sun shone brightly and dappled the road with interesting shadows as it peeked through the trees. The wind had picked up a bit overnight, and blossoms scattered in the breeze and tumbled across the pavement in an air dance as the branches shed their adornments.

When the mansion came into view, I felt a weird pang in my chest. There really was something about the place. I had wanted to explore it for years and was so excited when Dev told me that Roch had reached out to see if we could investigate it. It was strangely captivating and yet almost familiar in a bizarre sort of way. But under it all was a miasma of intrigue that I couldn't wait to delve into more.

I parked where I could and grabbed my gear. It looked like I was the first one to arrive, so I dug the key out of my bag and headed through the gate. I felt a shiver when I got onto the porch and looked over my shoulder. Nobody was there. Maybe the wind had hit me just right and tricked my nerves.

We'd found out the entire door was new, not just the gorgeous stained-glass window. Roch had told Dev they'd had to replace it because it'd randomly cracked and shattered when two of his tile guys were working in the foyer. One of the workers had gotten cut badly enough that he'd had to go to the emergency room for stitches. We'd been trying to come up with testable theories for that ever since and hadn't come up with anything definitive for why or how it'd happened.

The porch was too far away from the road for anything to have flown up from a car. Something from the tree could have hit the window just right. Or, given the time of year it happened, it could have just been temperature variances and pressure affecting a hairline crack already there. Who knew? We honestly weren't sure, but it went into our column of unexplained.

While the non-woo-woo folk on the team generally lived and died by the adage, *when in doubt, throw it out—*

something we'd actually copied-slash-borrowed from another well-known paranormal crew—we had to think outside the box. However, we didn't like to waste too much time debunking or having the psychically gifted research something stupid when there were always more exciting things to explore.

I walked into the parlor where the team had set up the command center and stashed my stuff near the desk in one of the plastic totes we'd brought in for just that. As I stood, I swore I saw movement out of the corner of my eye and turned, looking at the bank of computer monitors that Turner had brought in the last time I was here. Nobody had come in, and the drapes on the windows were closed.

I looked at the desk again. It appeared as if Van and Halen had been in at some point, too, since a bunch of their equipment sat near the soundboard. As I was inspecting a device I hadn't seen before, I saw something in my peripheral vision again and turned the other way, just barely catching movement in the reflection of one of the blank computer monitors. I turned more and tried to figure out what it might have been, but I didn't see anything.

My head started to pound more, and I moved to my bag to dig out some ibuprofen. Just as I tossed them back, the front door opened, and Dev and Hanlen walked in, Dev's blue nose pit bull terrier between them.

Mystique saw me and stopped, then wagged her tail and came bounding over. She knew me. And she loved me. I crouched and met her with a huge smile, accepting her little hops and doggie grunts and whines. She was such a sweet girl, but I had no idea why she was here. I gave her one last good rub behind the ears, kissed her on the forehead, and stood.

"Is it bring your daughter to work day?" I asked Dev.

Dev smiled, and Hanlen laughed. "It is, actually," he said. "I was going to tell you guys earlier, but we decided to surprise you instead. We've been training Myst to be an investigator."

"Oh. My. Goodness," I said. "Stop it. Are you serious? That's incredible. How does that work, though? I mean . . . I can see it totally being a great thing. She can smell critters in the walls. She can sense electromagnetic energy. This is fantastic."

Dev rolled his ocean-water-blue eyes and shook his head of silky curls, a grin on his lips. "Yes, she can do all of that. But she can also sense the spirits before we can. Sometimes, Lark can't tap in psychically right away, and they don't let me see them unless they *want* to be seen. Myst can sense them and alert us, especially if we think we're on to something already. And, yes, she can help you guys with all the science stuff, too." He pulled Hanlen close and gave her a one-arm hug. "Hanlen's been working tirelessly with her at the plantation since we moved in. We're going to use today and day one of filming as our trial runs to see how she does in real-world situations. During and since the Arborwood investigation, we've been getting her used to our ghost crew, and she's done really well."

Ah, yes, the "ghost crew."

He squatted and patted his knees. Myst propped her front paws on his lap and licked his face. "Yes, you have. You're a good girl, aren't you, baby?"

"I love it. I think it's brilliant. And not for nothing, but the viewers are going to go apeshit."

"I know, right?" Hanlen said, a huge grin splitting her beautiful face. She had her long brunette hair up in a ponytail today and it just highlighted her gorgeous amber eyes. "I said the same thing. I'd pick a ghost-hunting show with a beautiful, sweet dog over any of the competition any day. Especially *Ghost*—"

"Don't say it," Dev warned.

She raised a brow and quirked her lip. "What? Don't say that show headed by Z—"

"Don't you do it," he interrupted with a growl.

Hanlen winked and then patted him on the ass as she made her way over to me. "He's so salty with that one." She hitched a thumb over her shoulder. "Ever since he dissed him on national television."

"He took my job, Hanlen! He knew we were going through some shit and took Buckner Mansion right out from under us. He has an entire freaking country and beyond to work with. We're *Haunted New Orleans*. New. Orleans. Our area is in the show's godsdamn name. We do Louisiana and the occasional emergency out of state."

He closed his eyes and blew a breath out his nose.

"And he had the audacity to say—on national television —that we don't do things the *right* way. And then went on record in that interview saying that Van and Lennie stole tech from his guys. That's absolute bullshit. Aside from the things that every team on every show uses, all our stuff is custom. And his show doesn't even have engineers on staff. They outsource everything." He shook his head. "Uh-uh. We shall not speak his name. I really kinda want to hex him."

I laughed. It *was* pretty messed up, and the bromance was most definitely no more. They used to be friends. We all used to hang out with the cast and crew of a bunch of the major paranormal reality shows all the time when we found ourselves in the same areas or at conventions. Now, it was some weird feud, and it seemed to be spreading. Honestly, if anyone were to ask me for my opinion, I would say it was the fact that our contract got extended, and our ratings skyrocketed even more after Arborwood—and they were good to begin with. Jealousy was an interesting thing.

"You two should really just hug it out," I said and smirked when Dev shot me a glare.

Just as Hanlen and I fist-bumped, Pax walked in with a massive box of French doughnuts and a bunch of drinks. I rushed over to help.

"Geez, did you buy the entire place out?"

"Pretty much," he said and held out the stack for me to take the tray on top. I grabbed it, and we headed over to the table to set everything down. The cardboard had barely made contact with the surface before

I had the straw jammed in my mouth and took a huge gulp.

"Mmm, that's the stuff."

Pax snorted and popped the top on his black coffee before taking a sip. "It is pretty good. But I'm starving, and fully leaded on an empty stomach is never a great idea. When is everyone getting here?"

"They should be here soon," Hanlen said as she came in with Myst, Dev following close behind with Lennie and Van's new device in hand.

"Yeah, a couple of them just texted me," Dev agreed. "Go ahead and eat something, Padre. Nobody's gonna care."

Less than forty minutes later, the entire cast and crew was packed into the mansion's dining room, stuffing their faces with beignets and fueling with chicory coffee—or in some cases, tea. I would never understand the tea fascination. It was dirty water. I mean, I could make *tea* by putting some weeds from my front lawn in some hot water, popping in a packet of artificial sweetener, and calling it good. But . . . to each their own.

I'd stick to some good 'ol café au lait that stuck to my ribs. But then again, me drinking only cold coffee could be seen as bizarre by some. My mom thought I was addled. She told me that in her and Dad's day, drinking cold coffee would have been considered sacrilegious. That was what microwaves and stove-top percolators were for. My argument? It was like drinking mud from the Hell's Gate natural spa in New

Zealand. But as one of the most powerful natural healing places on Earth, that might actually be good for you. Radioactive sludge from Mr. Coffee seemed like Montezuma's Revenge waiting to happen. Just saying.

Harper filled us in on some of the research she was following up on regarding the house. Aaron and James took us through some of the things they had planned for filler shots and told us where they needed each of us and when they wanted to get some of the footage. Turner went over the locations of all the static and trail cameras so we knew what we'd be working with, and then Lennie and Van showed us the new gear. They called it the *JumpBox* as a nod to their namesake band, Van Halen, and a play on the fact that it might, indeed, scare the piss out of some people. I kind of appreciated that.

"Okay, so," Van said, "we started with the concept of Steve Huff's Wonder Box, the instrumental trans-communication device that scans radio frequencies and adds reverb, using the results to *supposedly* help spirits communicate easier during electronic voice phenomena sessions. Then, we tweaked it to be more tonally realistic to the ear so you could distinguish between male and female energies better." He explained some more.

I nodded, impressed by the technology, still not so sure about the application. From what I could gather, though, the super twins had enabled it to use a much larger sound bank to expand the possibilities, getting rid of all the clicking and static and feedback usually present with devices of that type along the way, and then also enhanced it to connect to an integrated tablet to show text output of what was being said and keep a log on the device's hard drive. As a team, we spent hours going over EVP recordings, trying to decipher what we may have heard—if anything. If Lennie's software and Van's hardware could cut that work in half *and* make it more interesting and pleasing for both us and the viewers, it would be amazing.

After that, we split into teams. Pax, Dakota, and I took the second floor to do our initial investigations and walk-throughs and let Dakota work her psychic mojo, whatever that entailed. Turner had mounted cameras there, complete with night vision for when things really got underway, but we'd also each have a Handycam.

Dev, Hanlen, and Myst took the bedroom suites on the ground floor with James.

Aaron went with Larken into the screwed-up back area so she could do what she needed to do with the chest in the storage space and get some impressions there.

Van and Lennie stayed in the control room with Turner to monitor the cameras and let us know if anything needed to be adjusted or if they saw or heard anything, and Harper took off to see to a couple of patients and continue her research on the house and its earlier inhabitants.

We'd pick a group to take the third floor and the attic later in the investigation.

"Everybody clear on what we need to do?" Dev asked, and we all nodded.

"I'm so excited to be involved from the start with this," Hanlen said as she squatted to give Myst some love. "And I can't believe those words just came out of my mouth." She laughed. "This time last year, I was in Texas and thought all of this was bullshit."

"Not too long ago, you almost *died*," Dev said, and we all looked at him. "What? It's true, and I don't think ignoring the fact is healthy. I'm sure if Harper were here, she'd agree with me. I'm grateful that everything that happened brought us together,"—he smiled at Hanlen—"but I could have done without the whole serial-killer-taking-my-girlfriend-hostage thing."

Hanlen stepped towards him and rose on tiptoe to give him a kiss. "I'm fine, babe. You were the hero. As always."

"Uh, actually," Dev said and looked at me, "Sky kinda saved the day. If she hadn't busted in, guns blazing—literally—who knows what might have happened?"

I blushed. I *had* done that. I could still feel myself kind of coming out of a trance when Dev gently pushed on my clenched hands to get me to lower the gun. The time between me rushing in and telling the bastard to freeze and that moment with Dev were kind of a blur. Though a few too many moments between Pax's and my initial visit to this house and that day were hazy. I was just glad that nobody had been hurt more seriously, and that we'd made it in time before the sadistic fucker had a chance to actually finish what he'd set out to do.

"Everyone good?" Birdie asked. "Make sure to protect yourselves, even though we shouldn't experience anything too major during the day. Still, the energy in this place is weird and definitely on the dark side, so you never know. And, as we've seen on occasion before, if it's strong enough, it doesn't matter if the sun is still up or not."

We *had* seen things during the day on occasion—stuff we weren't able to explain away. So, I would give her this one. This time. I looked around the room. I saw Dakota wringing her hands, and everyone else nodded in agreement before breaking off to grab what they needed to head to their respective spots.

This was when things got fun.

CHAPTER 4

~Paxton~

I followed the ladies up the grand staircase to the second floor, taking a right at the landing in the direction of the currently-under-construction master bedroom that took up the majority of the right wing. I'd been in there before. The space was beautiful with a cream and beige textured finish on the walls and opulent Victorian furnishings. They were still working on the fireplace and the crown molding, and the bathroom was still under construction, only the refinished copper tub in place currently.

Roch had said that his crew had smelled what reminded them of the sewer while in the suite. Had seen tools flying across the room. The window had come slamming down on one of the guy's hands as he tried to finish the trim, and at one point, two of the crew—guys who spent time together *off* the job—got into a fistfight so bad that one of them ended up at the hospital with a fractured eye socket.

When we entered the space, Dakota stopped short. "Whew, boy," she said and rubbed at her arms. "I wasn't in here the last time I stopped by. This room is thick."

I had to agree. It felt wrong. Even more so than the area down below by the crawl space, and that had set off my internal alarms, too. I glanced over at Sky to see her rubbing at her throat. I doubted she even realized she was doing it, but it was clear that the energy of the room affected her, too. I brushed a hand across my crucifix hidden under my shirts.

I grabbed the Handycam and made sure that the battery was fully charged. It often wasn't so bad during the day, but at night, in places that had residual energies—especially intelligent ones—haunts liked to drain the charge on electronics to muster enough energy to affect the realm of the living.

I started recording and did a pan of the space, making sure to get footage of the so-called hotspot areas. We likely wouldn't use it for the show unless something incredible happened, seeing as most of the reels for the final product outside of the glamour shots, the introduction, and the outro were night vision, but it was still our job to document anything we did for research purposes.

I focused on Dakota, who had taken a seat on the Queen Anne chair near the fireplace, her Handycam on the side table next to her, pointed her way. She was sitting quietly with her palms turned up on her thighs, eyes closed and breathing even. I knew that she was tapping into her psychic abilities to see what she could sense. Dakota wasn't as sensitive, and she didn't have the God-given power that Larken and Dev did, but she was a very gifted medium all the same.

When I shifted to take in the other side of the room, I caught Sky near the bathroom door, her Handycam in her non-dominant hand. She also had an EMF device out and was taking a reading of the space. I walked closer.

"Anything?" I asked.

She lifted the device. "It's weird. It's spiky and very inconsistent. The copper tub could have something to do with that, especially if there are magnetized pipes and things are grounded just right, but . . ." She rotated to take in the area to the right of the door, and I saw the meter drop to almost imperceptible levels. She then walked to the other side of the door near the armoire, facing away from the bathroom. "There's definitely something going on here." I looked at the device and saw that it was all the way in the red.

She rubbed at her throat again with the side of her thumb, the EMF device still clutched in her fingers. "Hey," I said, putting a hand on her shoulder. "Are you okay?"

"What?" She looked at me and then seemed to realize what she had been doing. "Oh. Oh, yeah, I'm fine. Just have a tickle or a lump or something. Maybe I didn't swallow the painkillers I took earlier well enough or I'm allergic to something up here."

I didn't think that was it at all, but I didn't push. I walked to the other side of the room and got some shots of that area and the massive walk-in closet—another place that Roch had said caused some issues with his crew—and then panned back over to Dakota before silently getting closer. I glanced over my shoulder to see that Sky had disappeared into the bathroom. I knew if she needed me to corroborate something, she'd holler, so I stayed where I was and watched Dakota.

She took a deep breath and then wiped her palms on her jeans. I noticed she looked a little tense, the skin around her eyes and mouth pinched a bit more than it should be, especially given she'd gone into her meditative state. She was fidgeting more, too, and generally didn't when she was working, so I figured it might be a good idea to check on her.

"Dakota. Everything okay?"

She took a deep breath through her nose and let it out slowly. With her eyes still closed, she answered. "I'm fine. But . . . I'm getting all sorts of stuff. Which is actually kind of strange given that it's still daytime. Means there is a whole lot going on here. And whatever it is has a ton of energy. There are two distinct entities in this room alone. Right now. One is a powerful male presence, very take-charge. Assertive. Maybe even aggressive. The other?" She shook her head. "I can't pin it down; it's slippery. But it sets off all my alarm bells. The voice in my head is sibilant. Seductive. Not right at all. And I think it might be speaking in tongues. It makes me feel sick to my stomach." She opened her eyes and pinned me with a stare. "We might be dealing with more than we bargained for here, Padre. Do you have your gear?"

I nodded and felt my stomach clench. When Birdie had come by a couple of weeks earlier, she'd immediately said that she felt as if at least one of the presences was on the dark side, but we hadn't had time to get more than that. Regardless, we were prepared to potentially encounter a malevolent entity. Figured we'd likely have to deal with some residual poltergeist activity as the crew had claimed. But an intelligent, non-human spirit was something altogether different —if that's what this was. We'd have to worry about oppression. Brace against possession. The skeptics in our cast and crew who didn't naturally shield against such things would be particularly vulnerable, even if their disbelief took some of the evil's power away.

Despite my sordid past with the Church and the loss of my collar after an unsanctioned exorcism— something that was one hundred percent necessary to save a child's life—I was still a recognized demonologist. I had the necessary educational background to do what needed to be done. I also had the inner strength, balance, and confidence. The archdiocese didn't like to claim me, but they didn't have a choice. I had proven myself as an expert in the field before things went south. Had been given permission by the Holy See to do what needed to be done. Despite the fact that they'd excommunicated me because of their backwards beliefs outside of the one that should matter—the belief in the Holy Trinity, and the safety of humankind and their souls—and I could no longer give or receive certain sacraments and couldn't perform major rites of exorcism, I could still do the blessings and minor exorcisms required. And I was still a recognized expert in the field. I had the piety, knowledge, prudence, and integrity of life to be deemed what they called a *lay faithful*, and thus able to perform minor rites and blessings.

And where the Church wouldn't dare to step in—which was often—or wasted too much time deciding if it was worth it for them—also often—I did. Still, I wasn't sure I was up for something big if that's what this ended up being. It had been a while since I had been in the thick of something really bad. I had contacts, of course, people I knew who could do what we might need and assist me in the rite of major exorcism if it came to that, but they were those I wasn't too keen on reaching out to. People from my past that I liked to keep buried as much as possible.

Thinking of the skeptics and nonbelievers on our team, I immediately thought of Sky and felt as if I should go and check on her. "You good?" I asked Dakota.

"Yeah, I'm gonna try and get some more, but I'm going to be careful. I don't even want to do any automatic writing in here. I don't feel safe without additional precautions. There's clearly already a doorway open. We don't need to let anything else in before we're ready. The boss and Birdie haven't done their thing with the property yet, setting the circle and opening the way, and we're not as protected as we probably should be."

"Be safe," I said and then nodded and headed to the bathroom. I panned the area with the camera and swore I saw something but figured it was probably just an optical illusion. But the camera had been on, so we'd review the footage later for any light anomalies.

Sky was in the corner by the tub, sitting on an upholstered bench that had been built into the corner of the walls with storage underneath, her Handycam propped near her. Her kit was open at her feet, and I saw her messing with something I didn't recognize. Trying not to startle her, I knocked a knuckle twice on the doorjamb.

Her head jerked up anyway, and her eyes went a little wide. "Sorry," I said. "Didn't mean to scare you. What's up?"

She looked back at the device in her hand. "I'm trying to check the electricity usage in here. This may not work because the outlets in here don't have anything drawing from them currently, but I still want to see. I'm all buzzy, and the EMF readings just keep getting more erratic."

The hairs on the back of my neck and arms were standing at attention, too, so I knew what she meant by *buzzy*. I wasn't so sure it had to do with electricity,

48

though. Or even static. There was something going on in here—and not just this room. The entire house.

She used the probes on the device to test three different outlets in separate areas and then just shook her head. "That's all completely normal, and they're all powered. Doesn't seem to be a short or a disturbance in the grounding or flow anywhere."

She walked over to the copper tub and went to put her hand on it. My breath hitched. I wasn't sure why. Maybe because we had just been talking about electricity, and she was about to touch a big conductor.

Just as she placed her hand on the lip of the tub, she bent at the waist, gasping. I nearly dropped the Handycam in an effort to get to her, knowing I needed to keep rolling in some capacity. When I reached her and put a hand on her neck, she straightened a little, her hands on her knees, her back flat. "Are you okay?" I asked.

She panted a bit. "Yeah. Yeah. Just . . . not sure."

"You didn't get electrocuted, did you?"

"What? No, no," she said, straightening, causing my hand to drop away. "Nothing like that. I just . . . got a little lightheaded. My vision started to close in for a minute, and it was a bit hard to breathe. I'm okay. Really. Probably should have had more than sugar for breakfast." She looked me in the eyes, her dark pools full of sincerity but her pupils a little blown. I knew she was all right, but I also saw the fatigue on her face. She'd tried to hide it with makeup, but like our first day here when it was just the two of us, I saw the dark circles under her eyes and the pallor of her skin.

I put a hand on her shoulder and saw her relax a little more. "You're really okay?"

"Yeah, I'm good." She nodded. "We should probably get back to Dakota."

She was right, but I hated what I'd just witnessed. My gut was telling me that something was going on here. Something that would only get worse as the sun sank into the horizon.

Something I wasn't sure any of us were prepared for.

CHAPTER 5

~Schuyler~

It was night one of filming, and I was excited to dive in, but also beyond exhausted. The two energy shots I'd taken earlier already felt as if they were wearing off, and we had a very long night ahead. I just couldn't seem to get a good night's sleep lately. I'd always been one that didn't remember my dreams, but I'd been recalling more and more of the ones I'd had recently. They were dark, full of blood, and downright terrifying. Which was saying something since I loved all things horror and immersed myself in anything creepy as often as I could.

But these . . . scenes of people in hooded cloaks surrounding an altar, chanting in a language I didn't understand. There was always a male figure at the head of the group, holding something that looked a lot like Birdie's athame—the ceremonial dagger that she used to set the magical, energetic circle before each of our investigations. There was always a chalice nearby, too, something big and ornate and ominous, and it only brought back bad memories of what'd happened at Arborwood and all the hell the team had experienced there.

Two nights ago, I'd even had visions of children. Blood and shadows and freaking Hell gates. Flashes of creatures with reptilian skin. Ghostly apparitions with pits for eyes. It was disturbing, and I had no idea where it was all coming from.

I really hoped that I wasn't losing it. Between feeling so crappy lately and these dreams, I was starting to worry that I had something seriously wrong. Perhaps there really was something environmentally toxic at Lamour. Maybe it was just burnout. I should think about talking to Harper. She wasn't only a kickass psychologist, she was also my friend, and I knew she'd be all too happy to listen and give me some advice.

Thinking of Harper had my mind shifting to the things she had uncovered about the house. After the actress and her husband had bought the place and lived out their lives there in the twenties, it had been owned by at least four different families who'd all seemingly left suddenly until it had been purchased by a guy who'd turned it into a sort of commune. From Harper's research, and what Dev said Burke had been able to uncover, thirteen people had called the mansion home from nearly the first day under his ownership, and at one point, eighteen people had lived there. When the guy died, he'd passed it on to his son, and the tradition had continued.

People had reported incidences of black masses, and on a fateful night thirty or so years ago, all twelve members of the so-called Moon Call Coven that currently lived in the house had died suspiciously, nearly taking the mansion with them in a fire. The place had sat empty ever since, only maintained enough for sustainability by the local historical society, with numerous business transactions falling through until the real estate mogul Roch worked for purchased the place twelve years ago.

They'd been trying to renovate the house for the last decade to turn it into a bed and breakfast with issue after issue, which had eventually led to Roch calling Dev for help. And so . . . here we were.

I pulled up to the curb and saw the team vans and Dev's and Pax's vehicles. It looked as if I was the last one to arrive. I glanced at the clock and saw that I was still early and breathed a sigh of relief. Given how out of it I'd been recently, I was afraid I had really screwed up.

The front door opened, and Pax stepped out onto the porch. "There she is." He smiled.

"Hey," I said and then grabbed my gear, making my way through the gate. Pax rushed down the porch steps to help me, taking some of the stuff from my hands and giving me a long look.

"What?" I said, feeling a little prickly.

"You all right?" he asked.

"Yeah. Fine. Just haven't been sleeping well is all. Everybody here?"

"Yep, they're all inside, getting ready. We'll head back out here so Birdie and Dev can do their thing and then dive in. Harper's not here tonight. Dev has her looking into more on the Moon Call Coven, seeing as it's been hard to glean information on what exactly happened with all of that. It's almost as if someone ordered a gag order or something. Anyway, she said she'd ring if she found anything useful."

"Good. That's good," I said and kept walking, feeling like I was moving through molasses. I knew Lark would probably give me hell. She'd take one look at me and know how beat I was. Something about the aura, or so she claimed. She'd warned me before about making myself vulnerable before an investigation, but given that I didn't give any of that much stock and had done official forensics investigations on much less sleep before, I consistently told her that I was okay and would be fine.

Pax held the door for me, and we entered the house to a cacophony of noise as the cast and crew all did their thing.

"Where do you want this?" Pax asked, and I took him in for the first time. He had on a blue-and-green-and-white-plaid button-down that brought out the color of his eyes, faded and distressed jeans, and his favorite black boots. He had his shirt open today over a bright white T-shirt, and his hair was spiked and artfully disheveled as always, pairing well with his forever-present scruff.

I got my mind back on track and answered. "Let's just set it down in the corner of the parlor if we can find some room in there. I'll shift what I need later if I have to."

We moved through the crowd, and I said my hellos, watching as everyone went through their pre-recording checks. The team worked like a well-oiled machine. Even with the losses we'd incurred recently, things still ran super smoothly.

I looked at the control desk and took in our newest addition as I set down my stuff. Turner was the youngest member of the cast and crew at only nineteen. He had light red hair and dark blue eyes and an easy-going demeanor. But he was smart. Like scary smart, having already graduated from college. He'd told us that he'd been homeschooled before university and thus ahead of most kids his age. I wondered why he was settling for being a tech grip on a TV show and not off doing something bigger, but I was sure he had his reasons. I didn't know much about him yet. All I knew was that we were lucky to have found him—or, more accurately, that *he'd* found us—and he fit in really well with the entire gang, though he'd taken a particular liking to Birdie. And, as was always the way with Lark, she became the team mother and babied him—to his obvious delight. If I didn't know better, I'd almost think they knew each other.

Dev and Hanlen walked in from the other archway, Birdie following behind with Myst. "The gang's all here," Hanlen said and smiled.

Dev pulled her close and kissed her temple. "Everybody ready?" he asked the room.

We all nodded and smiled and issued words of agreement.

"It should be dark in about an hour. Let's get outside, get the circle set, open the way, and get this show on the road." He beamed and then looked to his left. "Wren and Findley say the place is quiet right now, but Desmond said he doesn't think that will last long. He saw quite a bit of activity here last night. We could be in for an eventful evening."

This was one of those things that I just let happen. Wren, Findley, and Desmond were dead. Wren was Dev's sister, the one he'd lost to the serial murderer just over two years earlier. It was the RƎDRΩM case I'd consulted on for the NOLA PD. Findley was her fiancé, who'd died in a tragic accident after he found out that she had been murdered, and Desmond was a soldier from the War of 1812, who Dev used as a *runner*— whatever that entailed. I didn't pretend to understand and couldn't entirely wrap my head around any of it because my mind didn't work that way, but I usually just didn't think about it and focused on what I *could* explain. Besides, given that Lark and Dakota—and now even Hanlen—backed Dev up, and most of what they relayed from the *ghost crew* ended up being pretty damn accurate, I just let it be. It wasn't like I had much time to dwell on anything anyway. We were much too busy for that.

As I was about to turn to grab what I'd need for what we were about to do outside, I noticed something move out of the corner of my eye. It was in the same location as where I'd sworn I had seen something the other day—back behind the monitors. I turned, once again looking for something that could have caused it, but I didn't see anything. I really hoped that my exhaustion wouldn't make me mess this up. This was a big show for *Haunted New Orleans*, and it meant a lot to me personally, too, given my fascination with the place. I needed to get my shit together.

About two hours later, Birdie had us all protected in sacred space with help from her gods, goddesses, ancestors, and guides—another thing I didn't even pretend to understand—and had handed off blessed and charged crystals for each of us to carry. Dev had opened the way, beseeching the lwas—the primary spirits of Vodou as he'd told us—to assist in our investigation. Given the things that Lark and Dakota had experienced already at Lamour, they'd also had Paxton say a prayer and do a blessing for us before they closed the circle. It was all just words to me, but I loved these people enough to respect what made *them* feel safe. Now, we were all inside, about to break off into groups to start the real investigation and get filming for night one.

"Hey, Sky?" Dev called, and I turned to find him in the foyer.

"Yeah, boss?"

"I need to take Hanlen and Birdie with me to do a blind spirit box session in the back area with Aaron like we did at Arborwood. Do you want to take Myst and Padre and head up to the third floor and the attic if you have time? I need Dakota to do some work in the bedroom down here, but you guys should be fine and can take Myst on a test run."

"I'm good with that, but what do I need to do with her?"

"You shouldn't have to do anything. Just have her with you. If she senses something, she will alert you. Watch her coat. If you see her fur rise, she's likely on to something. If she points or sits or alerts by barking or chuffing or growling, you guys can check it out more."

"Sounds good." I dropped down and patted my knee for Mystique, and she came bounding over, her doggie tongue lolling. "You ready to do some work, good girl?" She licked my hand, and I stood just as Pax walked up with one of my kits and his Handycam slung over his shoulder. He handed me the JumpBox. I looked at Dev.

"You want us to use the new device?" I asked.

"Absolutely," he said. "None of us needs it right now, and since we haven't done much exploring on the upper levels, it'll be nice to get some data."

My stomach flipped. "This is awesome. I'm so excited to try it. The super twins are freaking amazing with their technology, and it'll be interesting to see if it can work in a real-world test. I mean, can you imagine the metrics we can go through later?"

Dev laughed. "All right, you nerd. Get to it." He raised his head and did a quick pan, taking everyone in. "Good luck tonight, guys. Stay vigilant, be safe. Let's try and make some history. Keep your walkies on. Let's reconvene at"—he checked his smartwatch—"midnight. We'll swap locations and get ready for the witching hour."

As all supernatural shows would tell you, the so-called witching hour was three a.m. Normal *spectral* activity was good for any time after dark—and even sometimes during the day if it was particularly powerful—but dark energy was, for some reason, anticipated and documented to be the most active at or around three in the morning. As Pax had informed the team, it was a way for the dark forces to mock the time that Jesus died on the cross, which apparently happened to be at three in the afternoon. He'd also told us that everything dark-entity related generally came in threes—something about the Holy Trinity or something. If we started seeing that pattern, we needed to be more aware. I guessed we'd see.

"Lights out," Hanlen called, and I heard her chuckle. It was probably weird for her to go from skeptical non-believer to cast member in such a short time, but she was taking to it really well.

Pax and I started out and secured our gear just as someone killed the lights. Once we had everything in place, we headed for the stairs. I sent Mystique up ahead of us and told her to wait, and then we followed, panning the area for anything we might be able to use later. I still had the same buzzy, alert, uneasy feeling I'd had every time I'd been in the house and wondered what the night had in store.

We'd soon find out.

CHAPTER 6

~Paxton~

I followed Sky up the stairs, getting a shot of Myst sitting on the landing and waiting for us, panting happily. It would be fun to see how she reacted to things during the investigation. I loved that Dev and Hanlen had trained her to be an investigator, and I was excited that Sky and I got to take her on her inaugural look-see.

I panned around, taking in the areas on either side of the grand, split staircase. I still felt odd, and it always felt as if someone were watching me. It bothered me, and my senses were on high alert. For some reason, I had decided to don my charm of Our Lady of Mount Carmel tonight, a miniature of the habit that the monks wore as a sign of their love and devotion to the

Holy Mother. I didn't usually wear anything but my Saint Michael medallion or my crucifix, but something had told me to wear the Brown Scapular tonight, and it made me feel more comfortable. The charm represented the relationship between Jesus and the Virgin Mary, and was said to be one of the strongest weapons against Satan ever. Like most things, a lot of that was faith, but still . . .

Mine was simple and unassuming, a twisted rope of brown material and leather worn over the shoulders and clasped at the neck like a backwards necklace, with a brown wool tab at the nape, sporting a gold-embroidered cross. It had belonged to my grandfather and had been blessed by the Pope himself. My father hadn't wanted me to have it, but he didn't have much choice since Grandda had left it to me in his will.

We took the hallway to the back and were about to ascend the stairs to the third floor when I heard something.

"Did you hear that?" I asked Sky.

She had already turned in the direction I had. "I did," she said.

"It sounded like . . . knocking, right?

"Or footsteps." She looked up at the ceiling, just as Myst was doing. "Nobody's upstairs, right?"

"Nope. I don't even think anybody's on the second floor but us."

The sound came again, a trio of thumps, and we looked at each other, my camera taking in her raised eyebrow.

"Okay, we have activity. I can almost guarantee the camera picked that up." I moved closer to Sky, and just as I was about to say that we should head on up, the sound of an exhale and a growl came from nowhere, yet was somehow somewhere in the space between us.

"What the fuck?" Sky exclaimed and jumped back. She looked at me and then Myst, who hadn't moved, but the hair down the center of the dog's back stood at attention. I could relate. The hairs on my neck and arms were doing the same. "That was a growl, right?"

"I heard what sounded like a growl and a breath. Whatever it was, I think Myst heard it, too. And I don't think it was her."

"I heard it also," James said as he walked up the stairs behind us, the big camera perched on his shoulder.

"Hey, man," I said. "I'm glad you're here. We could use some more footage, especially since we only have the one Handycam."

He nodded. "Yeah, Dakota didn't need me and had her mini-VR so Dev sent me up here with you guys. Looks like I picked the perfect time to show."

Sky nodded and then looked down at Mystique before crouching and putting a hand on the dog's neck. Myst whined a little, but otherwise seemed okay.

Sky stood again, readjusted her pack slung across her chest, and looked at me, her dark eyes and hair glowing brightly in the night vision of my camera.

"After you," I said and motioned for her to go down the hall first. I readjusted the bag over my shoulder and followed, Myst walking between us, and James bringing up the rear.

When we got to the door at the end of the hall that opened to the third-floor stairwell, my stomach churned. I wasn't sure why, but something wasn't quite right. Just as I had the thought, Myst sat and growled at the door. Sky turned around to look at the pit bull and then turned her gaze to James and me.

"I'd say that's a sign."

"Yep," I agreed.

"Do you think we should bust out the JumpBox here and get some EMF readings before even going up the stairs, and give the new device a try for the camera?"

"Given Myst's reaction," I said, "it probably wouldn't be a bad idea." I set my bag down and rummaged in Sky's for the JumpBox and the K2 meter. I handed the meter to her and then fired up the super twins' invention, letting it boot up.

"EMF is kinda high here," she said. "We're pretty steady at over one-point-five." She walked a bit to the right and then skirted me and walked to the left. "It's not consistent, though. Same as it was in the bedroom the other day." She looked around the area with her mini-flashlight. "I don't see anything environmental that could be contributing to a spike like that, but we can look into it some more tomorrow when it's light out."

The device came online and emitted a soft chime. Myst barked, and I looked at her. "It's okay, girl. That was just me." I paused. "*If* you were barking at that." I looked at Sky, and she shrugged. I handed her the device as soon as she put the K2 meter on the floor, propped up on its stand.

"Okay," I said and focused the Handycam on Sky and the JumpBox. "Is there anybody here with us?" I asked, looking around the space and panning my camera to catch anything that might happen. Just as I was almost back to Sky, a feminine-sounding voice from the device spoke up.

"*Yes.*"

I moved a little closer and peeked at the tablet integrated into the JumpBox, seeing that the word YES was on the screen, and the blinking cursor was now on the line below it.

"Okay," Sky said. "This is really freaking cool." She smiled, and I grinned in return. It really was.

"Who are we speaking to?" I asked.

"—*ko,*" came that same feminine voice from the machine.

"What did that register as on the screen?" I asked Sky.

"It didn't really get it. It shows as an ellipsis and then a *K* and an *O*. Which, is actually what we heard, so I'd say Lennie did a damn good job with the software."

I had to agree. But I really wanted to know who we were talking to. "Can you repeat that, please? Who do we have the pleasure of talking to tonight?"

There were some incoherent words from the device

along with some bleeps and blarts, and then a completely silent pause before, "*Mother. Píngguǒ.*"

"You're a mother?" Sky asked and then looked at me. "What was that second word? The tablet couldn't really make sense of it."

"I'm not sure," I said. "It almost sounded like another language. Try to get some more."

"Whose mother?" Sky asked. "Someone who lived here before?"

"*No,*" answered the voice.

"No, you're not a mother?" I asked, a bit confused.

"*No, leave . . . alone. Need t—help.*"

Just as I was about to ask another question, a new voice came through the JumpBox. This one distinctly male.

"*Shut up, bitch.*"

"*Help,*" came the feminine voice again.

"*Mine,*" answered the male presence—at least, I *thought* it was the same voice—and the authority in the word, even with the distortion and through the device, made my heart rate pick up.

Seemed we had some conflicting energies tonight.

I took in Sky's curious expression and then peeked at James to see him shaking his head.

And the night had only just begun.

CHAPTER 7

~Schuyler~

*W*ell, this was interesting. I peeked at the tablet screen again to see the word that had come through after *Mother*. When Pax had said that it sounded like another language, it'd sparked something in my memory. *PÍNGGUǑ* was the word on the screen. I flashed back to a conversation I'd had with my mom after I'd gotten my tattoo. She'd gotten flustered that I'd done it that she'd slipped from English to Mandarin a couple of times and had said what'd sounded like, peeng go-ah. Looking at the word on the tablet, even with the accents—which I assumed were right since Lennie really was kind of a genius—I thought that might be it.

"I think that word we couldn't figure out, the one

the feminine voice said after *Mother,* might be in Mandarin. I actually think it's *apple,*" I said. "I remember my mom using it after I got my tattoo."

"Hold up," James chimed in. "You have a tattoo? Of an *apple?*"

I looked at him and raised an eyebrow. "Not the time, dude." I shook my head. "Anyway, I don't speak Mandarin Chinese, but I'm almost certain that could be it. Mom slips into it quite frequently when she's excited or flustered, and I've learned to pick up enough to at least recognize it. What in the world could it mean?"

"Who knows?" Pax said. "But I think we need to keep going." He looked at his watch. "It's already nearing ten and we haven't done much investigating. We need to see what's on the third level and try to at least make it up to the attic if at all possible."

I agreed, so I made sure that Myst was good and headed up the stairs. Like the second story, the third floor had four bedrooms. I assumed that two had en suite bathrooms, and the other two shared the one that was situated between them. That door was the only one currently open, and I walked towards it.

The inside was basic white with a bit of black. A white-tile floor with tiny black diamonds, a white pedestal sink, hanging white cabinet mirror, and a small, freestanding vanity desk off to the side. The other side of the space was occupied by a white, claw-foot tub with a suspended shower curtain and a water-fall showerhead mounted to the ceiling, the controls of which were on the wall.

It didn't look interesting enough to investigate but I made sure both the guys got footage of it anyway.

We moved down the hall to the room on the end, and Myst immediately sat and pointed, her hackles raised.

"What's up, girl?" I asked and bent down to rub a hand down her back. She looked over her shoulder at me and whined. I glanced at the guys. "Seems we may have found another hotspot for something."

I dug out the K2 meter and took some EMF readings. They were elevated here, as well. I tried to orient myself and figure out where I was in regard to the second story and the ground floor and realized I had to be directly over the room with the copper tub, which was directly over the butler's pantry off the kitchen. Ironically—or maybe not so ironically if it ended up all being environmental—all of those areas were full of activity according to Roch and his guys. I told James and Pax as much.

"Likely not a coincidence," Pax said and moved even with me. "Care if I go first?"

"Be my guest," I said. It'd probably be best for him to do it anyway seeing as he had the Handycam. James could bring up the rear again.

Paxton opened the door and took one step into the room before stopping cold.

"What is it?" I asked.

"Do you hear that?" he said.

I listened a little more carefully and did, indeed, hear something. Insistent buzzing. "What is that?"

Pax walked a few more steps into the room and swept his camera left and right, holding out a hand to tell us to stay back. There were two floor-to-ceiling windows on the far side of the room to our left, and another on the wall perpendicular to it. The streetlight from outside shone directly in the single window on that wall, highlighting a mess of flies that I could see buzzing around and bumping into the glass and each other, even from where I stood.

"Ew," I said. "What's with all the insect activity?"

"I don't know," Pax answered. "But that might be what set Myst off."

He had a point. Maybe this wasn't a hotbed of the paranormal, after all. Perhaps she'd just been upset by the bugs. Then again, why were there so many flies in here to begin with?

"Wait there a second," Pax said as he walked even farther into the room, Myst following on his heels. James and I stayed in the hall just outside the door. I kept checking the K2 meter, and James had his camera pointed in the room, taking in Pax's journey across the expanse to the window.

He skirted the one twin bed jutting out into the room and then nearly brushed the armoire that separated the two windows on the far wall. Another bed sat in front of the buzzing horde, its long side about three feet from the window and the headboard against the half-wall the room shared with the closet. A vanity desk took up the area in the corner.

Just as Pax reached the window, the door in front of us slammed closed, nearly busting James's camera.

"Holy shit," he said and jumped back.

"What the fuck?" I yelled, immediately reaching for the knob. It wouldn't turn. I spun to James to see him shaking his head but doing his job and keeping the camera rolling. I rattled the knob again but felt no give. I pounded on the wood.

"Pax? Paxton. Are you okay? Open up. What the hell just happened? Did you open the window?" I couldn't hear anything from inside, and that worried me. I rattled the knob one more time with the same result and decided to try shoving my side against the door while pushing. Maybe the thing had warped. I did that a few times but didn't get any results besides a sore shoulder. I turned to James.

"Can you put the camera down for a second and try? I don't like this."

James did as I asked, propping the camera on a narrow table along the hallway wall, and tried to get the door open. "It feels locked," he said. "I wonder if it engaged when the door shut. But *how* did it shut? It didn't just gently close, it freaking slammed and almost took my damn head off."

"I know," I said and pounded on the door again as James retrieved the camera. "Pax, can you hear me?" Nothing. I pressed my ear to the door and tried to listen. It was strange that Myst wasn't barking. If nothing else, the slam of the door should have startled her enough to make her speak up. And us pounding and calling should have agitated her, too.

Not sure what else to do, I woke the JumpBox from its hibernation and decided to see if I could get anything. Which was ridiculous. What help could it provide?

"Is anybody here?" I rolled my eyes.

"Here," came that same feminine voice from before.

I shrugged and glanced at James. "What's going on?" I asked, feeling a hundred kinds of ridiculous for trying to get answers about a defective door from a disembodied voice in a piece of technology.

"He has him."

"Well, *that's* not ominous at all," James said, and I glared at him.

"Not helpful, dude." I looked back at the device. "Who has him?" I asked.

"Leave. Now. Not safe," the voice said, and I felt a chill race down my spine.

"Now can I say it's ominous?" James chimed in.

"Seriously?" I shot him a look.

I grabbed my walkie from my belt and raised it to my face, just about to press the talk button, when the door creaked open. I frowned and glanced at James, who raised an eyebrow and shrugged in reply. I slowly pushed open the door and peeked inside to see both Pax and Myst standing stock-still near the window on the right, both their forms highlighted by the moonlight, creating striking silhouettes.

"Pax?" I called, but he didn't reply. I glanced over

my shoulder at James. "Follow me." I saw him nod, and then I walked into the room, looking around. I didn't see anything, and Pax and Myst remained motionless on the other side of the second bed. My heart rate kicked up, and a cold sweat broke out across my body. I was terrified. Not for me, but for Paxton. I couldn't explain why, but I didn't want to imagine anything happening to him, and I just needed to know that he was okay.

I gently reached out and touched the back of his shoulder. He jerked a bit and then turned to me.

"I thought I told you to wait a minute."

I just stared at him for a second to see if he'd say more. When he didn't, I looked at Myst, who was still staring straight ahead at the window, no movement visible. I checked to make sure that James was still filming and then looked back at Paxton.

"Uh, I did wait, Pax. The door slammed, and we've been trying to get into you guys for quite a while now. What the hell happened?"

His brow furrowed. "What do you mean? We just got in here a second ago. The flies are bad, and I was trying to figure out what was causing them to congre-gate when Myst"—he reached down and touched her head, and she seemed to snap out of whatever was going on with her, though he didn't seem to notice— "alerted to something. I was just about to take a closer look when you came in."

What the hell? He didn't seem to have any memory of what'd gone on in the time that James and I had been locked out in the hall. Was there a gas leak in here or something? I turned to Myst and saw her lying on the floor, her head between her front paws, whining softly. It looked as if she didn't know what'd happened either, but it was clear that she knew that *something* wasn't right.

Just as I ran my hand from the back of Pax's shoulder down his arm and took a step closer to the window, the device I didn't realize was still on bleeped, and that same voice came through once more.

"Leave. Leave now."

Then, another voice, this one different than the male one from before and way more seductive, said, *"Oh, no. Stay. Be my guest."*

That gave me chills. "What the fuck?" I said. "Is someone downstairs messing with us?"

"Not likely." James shook his head, and I turned back to the window.

"What in God's name is going on?" Pax asked, just when James's walkie beeped as he pushed through to connect.

"Uh, boss? I think you should come to the third level. Now."

CHAPTER 8

~Paxton~

*I*t was the morning of day two, and we were all congregated around the mansion's dining room table, sucking down coffee and tea and waiting for Harper to show. She'd called Dev as we wrapped things up last night and said she had some information.

I didn't love being back here after what had happened, but this was my job, and I knew I was protected—most of us were. That didn't hold true for everyone, but we were professionals and knew what we were dealing with and potentially getting ourselves into.

We didn't even get to finish out the full investigation for day one because of what'd happened to us on the third floor. From what I'd been told, I'd lost at least fifteen minutes of time. When Dev and Hanlen came up to talk with us after James radioed down, we'd investigated the flies on the bedroom window and couldn't find a logical environmental explanation for them. It was a well-known fact that locations with purported demonic activity had insect infestations—among other things. There was a reason that scene existed in *The Amityville Horror*. And given the nasty voice we'd heard come out of the JumpBox, I wouldn't doubt one bit if we were dealing with a negative diabolical intelligence.

Seemed Dakota had tapped into one of the malevolent presences she'd felt the first night in the second-story bedroom, too. It'd told her to get the hell out and take the faithful with her this time. That there was no room in this house for anyone who didn't bow to the dark one—whatever that meant.

Dev, Hanlen, and Lark had gotten some great results during their spirit box session. They'd told us they'd heard from who they believed was the starlet from the twenties and from at least two other spirits they thought used to live in the house, and Dev had seen what he suspected was one of the witches from the Moon Call Coven, though she hadn't said anything. They'd gathered as much information as they could, and would have Harper and Burke dig into it more.

As much as I adored Harper and gave a nod to her excellent investigative skills, among the other things she brought to the team, Burke had an edge. After all, he was a ghost and wasn't constrained by the trappings of the mortal coil, and he'd been one heck of a historian before he died. The two of them made a unique yet excellent research pair.

And, apparently, Dev's cousin, Reagan, had become Burke's constant companion, helping in ways that none of us ever expected. Despite the tragedies that had taken them from us, we found solace in having them back in our lives again in some capacity. I envied Dev and Lark and Dakota the ability to communicate with them, but knowing they were around and happy was a balm despite how it went against my earliest beliefs that all souls either went to Heaven or Hell. My fallout with the Church had changed a lot about me. As had things with my family.

Not to mention, working with the show all these years had made me adapt, and I felt as if I were a more rounded individual for it—and maybe even more spiritual.

I felt a light touch on my shoulder and looked up to see Sky standing over me. I'd been so deep in thought; I hadn't realized she'd returned from the bathroom.

"How are you holding up?" she asked as she put a little pressure on my shoulder.

"I'm fine. How are you?"

"Exhausted," she said on a yawn and took the chair next to me, leaving her hand in place. For some reason, the events of the night before still weighed heavily on me, but her touch grounded me a bit. I reached up across my chest and put my hand over hers, squeezing her fingers gently.

I may not be able to remember exactly what'd happened, but I knew that something had, and it bothered me that I didn't know what had gone on with me and Myst during those fifteen minutes. When James and Sky had described how they'd gotten inexplicably locked out and that we'd almost been in a trance when they finally found their way back in, it reminded me of the research I'd done when studying to become a demonologist, and how inhuman entities could effectively put people into a psychic sleep. I wondered if that could happen while a person was awake. I'd have to look into it more if I could find the time.

I peered into Sky's dark, soulful eyes and smiled. She returned the expression and then slid her hand down my back before grabbing her coffee. The minute her hand fell away, I felt it in my soul. It was if she lit a place that had been cast into darkness. The things I felt for her were growing, but we had bigger fish to fry.

I shook my head and focused on the conversation happening around the table. Dev and Hanlen were feeding pieces of bacon to Myst while talking about the spirit box session and the women they'd contacted. They said the dog had earned a special treat after what she'd gone through the night before, and I had to agree. I'd buy her a Porterhouse if Dev would let me. Part of me wondered if things would have been worse for me if I hadn't had Mystique with me. I wasn't sure what made me think that, but like children, animals were inherently innocent. While evil forces wanted to possess that, they also didn't know what to do with it. It was harder for a demon or malevolent spirit to affect someone or something that didn't leave an opening for them to do so.

Just as I was about to ask for more information, I heard a quiet knock on the front door before it opened, and Harper walked in with her daughter. Harper had never brought Elliott with her before, so I wondered what was going on. I hoped it wasn't anything bad.

"Hey, honey," she said to her daughter and bent to be at eye level with her. "Why don't you go into the room over there and play with your dolly? I'll come and get you in a little bit after I talk to my friends."

"Okay, Mommy," the little girl said and ran off, a big smile on her face.

Harper walked the rest of the way to us, rubbing a hand down her cheek. "Hey, guys. Sorry about that." She pointed to the room that Elliott now played in. "My friggin' ex decided that she was too busy with her new boyfriend to watch our child and dropped her off unexpectedly at the house this morning when she was supposed to have her for another two days. I didn't have a babysitter set up and absolutely had to come and give you guys this information, so I had no choice but to bring her with." She glanced at Dev. "I'm sorry."

Dev got up and rounded the table, pulling Harper in for a hug. She melted into him and sighed. "It's okay," he said. "It's daylight, and the place is warded. We're fine." He stepped back and gestured to the table. "Do you want some coffee? You look like you could use some."

Harper sighed again. "You have no idea. I nearly pulled an all-nighter like you guys did with this, and when the doorbell rang at six-thirty, and I saw Sharon on the other side, I panicked. Luckily, when I opened the door, an adorable little girl tackle-hugged my legs, but I think it knocked ten years off my life—seeing Sharon at my place unexpectedly like that. I need caffeine like I need air right now."

She sat and poured herself a cup from the insulated takeout box, doctoring it and then taking a huge gulp. "Ahh, better already." She smiled and then reached into her bag, pulling out a stack of folders and passing them around the table.

"Okay, what you're looking at here is a compilation of research that I did, and some follow-up stuff on things that Dev told me Burke uncovered. Some of this is huge, guys. It may totally change how you proceed with the investigation."

I opened the folder and flipped through some of the printouts. I saw some stuff about missing persons cases, and other things about Moon Call that we already kind of knew about. I also saw some photocopied newspaper clippings of microfiched articles on the starlet and her husband who'd lived here. Seemed they had a bit of a speakeasy going and held drunken séances. No wonder the house was a hotbed of activity. Who knew how many supernatural doorways they'd opened and never closed? It may have even drawn the darker energies of the man who'd ended up creating the compound here that'd eventually become the black witch coven that'd been passed down for at least one generation that we knew of.

I flipped through some more pages, and my blood turned to ice in my veins. All the conversation around the table became a dull roar as my head pounded in time with my heart, and my gaze zeroed in on the name and picture on one of the last pages of research. *Father Dougal McGuire.* The scholarly article detailed how the Irish priest had been arrested in conjunction with the events in this house that'd ended in the fire and the deaths of nearly the entire Moon Call Coven. They'd ultimately let him go due to lack of evidence. He had then disappeared for a time, only to die tragically a decade later before he could be *brought to justice* —as so many thought he should be. People believed that he'd either taken his life out of guilt or died in some media-frenzy tragedy.

We'd looked into the events before, checking all public documentation we could easily find, but it had been nearly impossible to uncover the name of the priest for some reason, and the specific details surrounding the deaths and events was always muddy, as well. Now, I knew who it was thanks to Harper and Burke, and I wasn't sure what to do with the information. It didn't fit with anything in my head. Didn't align with any of my memories of that time, and I didn't know how to reconcile that fact. As I was thinking on that, Harper's words shook me out of my reverie and made those thoughts float to the back of my mind, at least for the moment.

"So, Lillian Scott, the actress who lived here, was apparently a gifted medium and performed all sorts of séances. I'm sure that's when all the nonsense here started. And then, as you'll see in the police reports I included, at least one member of three of the four families who lived here after that, disappeared. Padre can help confirm this,"—she looked at me—"but it seems that when an inhuman entity progresses from oppression to possession, it can result in one of two things in the last stages. Either spontaneous combustion or complete dispersion, which leads to the person just . . . poofing. Right?"

She wasn't wrong. The well-known demonologist, Ed Warren, had even written about it in one of his books. "That's the working theory, yes. I've read about it, too, and it did come up in my exorcism training. Combustion is rare. I think it's only been documented like three times in all of history. But once the case goes through oppression and possession, the person is effectively owned by the demon. Their personality is gone, and their soul is taken. The thought is that they're somehow dragged to Hell, which results in them disappearing altogether since the body cannot exist without the soul. Some reported it as it appearing as if the people were being swallowed by shadows until the darkness dissipated, only to leave no trace of the person behind. But none of that could ever be proven because those people were also affected and deemed slightly addled if not downright clinically insane—also likely a result of the oppression."

Harper grinned widely. "See! I think that's what happened to those homeowners. I think we might be dealing with an inhuman entity here, folks. You know I'm still skeptical about some of this stuff, but I was a good church-going child and I remember everything I was taught in Sunday school. Lillian opened the door for it or them to step through, they gained strength by oppressing and possessing the following homeowners, and then the coven gave it even more strength by worshipping it. Now, it has a foothold and won't let go. And given the dark stuff that went down here over the years, it's a very welcoming place for it."

"Are you serious?" Sky said. "You actually want me to believe that?" She took a breath. "You know, I used to kind of like this place. I mean, it's beautiful. Now, I just want to be done with it. This shit is ridiculous."

I understood her frustration, though I didn't like the tone of her voice. It didn't seem quite . . . Sky. Still, this was probably harder for her than most. She didn't believe in God. Belief like that had to be well-rounded. If you believed in a higher power, you had to believe in the darker side of things and vice versa. She seemed to be coming around a little because of the irrefutable things she'd seen and experienced while working with *Haunted New Orleans,* especially after what'd happened at Arborwood, but that didn't mean she liked it or really *grasped* it. Therefore, it took a toll.

"Well, okay, then," Dev said and blew out a breath. "I

mean, we kind of knew that what we were dealing with wasn't all fun and fluffy, but getting confirmation that it's inhuman is a bit concerning. Especially given what went down last night."

"Wait," Harper said. "What happened last night?"

Dev filled her in. I glanced over at Sky. She had her hair loose this morning, and the silky, black strands tickled my arm where she sat so close to me at the table. Her Japanese cherry blossom scent filled my nose and warmed something in my chest. I remembered when Lark had gotten her the lotion for Christmas one year for our office Secret Santa exchange. She'd loved it so much, she'd never stopped wearing it.

When Dev called on her to fill Harper in on what the spirits had said through the JumpBox and what exactly she and James had experienced upstairs, she straightened and tackled her job like she did everything. With passion. But I saw the tension in her. When she finished, I leaned in and whispered in her ear.

"Why don't you go and check on Elliott? Take a breather. We'll be fine without you for a minute, and I can fill you in on anything you need to know later."

She looked at me, her gaze locking with mine, and I saw the relief pass over her face. "Yeah." She nodded. "Yeah, that's a really good idea. I haven't been feeling myself lately and this is a bit much. Thank you." She leaned in and bussed my cheek with a kiss, something she'd done with others before but never with me, and then called over her shoulder that she was going to check on Elliott as she left the room.

I felt the heat of her lips linger. Forcing myself to be in the moment, I tried to focus on what was being said at the table.

Between the events of last night, what I'd just read in that folder, and how tied up I felt when it came to Sky, it would be a very, very long day. And I still needed to stop by the soup kitchen and make sure everything was running smoothly in my absence before I came back for night-two filming.

CHAPTER 9

~Schuyler~

I walked down the hall taking in the beauty around me. With everything that had been going on, the wonder of the place had almost disappeared into the background. Despite the strangeness of the investigation, I still loved this house. I entered the receiving room but stopped at the doorway, watching Elliott sitting on the floor, playing with her doll. I heard her giggling and mumbling, but I couldn't tell what she was saying.

"I know," she said and giggled again. "I know, but my mommy won't like that."

I frowned. I wondered if she was playing with an imaginary friend or something. I watched her for a little while longer.

"No. I don't really like it here. I don't think I want to stay. I like where I live."

I walked up, took a seat on the edge of the settee next to her, and smoothed her hair.

"Hi, pretty girl," I said.

She looked at me, her big brown eyes full of wonder. "Hi."

"I like your doll."

"Thank you," she said and smoothed the doll's hair as I had done with hers.

"Who were you playing with?" I asked.

"Huh?" She frowned and continued making her doll dance.

"When I walked in, you were talking to someone. Were you playing with someone? Do you have a friend?"

"Oh. Yeah, she's my friend."

"That's nice," I said. "What's your dolly's name?" I asked.

"It's, um . . . Her name's KoKo."

"KoKo. That's cute. Want to know something interesting?"

She turned to me, her eyes big and wide as if I were about to tell her the secrets of the universe. "Yeah." She drew out the word.

"There's someone here who has a name kind of like that, too," I said, thinking of our JumpBox session last night and the voice that'd claimed their name ended with a *ko* sound.

Elliott frowned, and I wondered what I'd said

wrong.

"Oh, I already know that." She twisted her lips. "I thought you were gonna tell me something else."

Now, it was my turn to frown. "Honey, how do you know that?"

"Because Seiko's my friend, silly. I was just talking to her and her boyfriend. I told you that," she said, as if it were the most natural thing in the world and she *had* told me that. And then she jumped up and ran off as if nothing had happened at all, leaving me sitting there slack-jawed.

What the hell?

That had to be a coincidence, right?

* * *

I HADN'T GOTTEN any rest as I'd hoped. I'd spent most of the day digging into the name Seiko and the Mandarin *apple* reference, but the only thing I could uncover was that they both had Chinese origins. I'd left my mom and dad a voicemail message to see if maybe they knew anything about it, but I hadn't heard anything from them yet. It was a weekday. Dad was probably in court, and Mom likely had a full docket of flower arrangements to get out. Her shop, Earth to Sky, had been doing really well lately, and I hoped it kept up for Mom. She loved her job, adored playing with plants and flowers, and I figured she'd do it until her hands no longer let her.

As backup, I also sent Harper a text to see if she

could add it to her list of research and let me know what she found—if anything.

I checked my watch. I had a few hours before I had to be back at the mansion for day two shooting. I was so drained, all I wanted was a couple of hours of sleep. Just as I stepped off the curb outside the library to head to my car, my phone buzzed. I pulled it out of my back pocket. It was Paxton.

"Hey, what's up?" I heard commotion in the background.

"Thank God you answered," he said. "It's a madhouse here at the kitchen, and I can't leave. I was wondering if you might be able to run by my place and grab me a change of clothes. I have like a quarter of a pot of stew on me right now thanks to one of our regular's kids, and I'm not going to be able to get home before I have to head back to the mansion."

There went my afternoon nap, but I would totally do this for him. "Sure. But . . . how am I going to get in?" I asked.

"There's a hidden key. If you take three steps from the porch, one of the bricks in the walk is a slightly different shade. It's loose. Just pry it up. The key's underneath."

"Nice," I said and smiled. Mine was in a flowerpot near the door. Not exactly rocket science if someone wanted to find it and get in. "I'm just leaving the library now so I'm close. Any requests for an outfit?"

"Well, since we're supposed to keep the same sorts of outfits for filming in case they need to do scene splices, I think I'm going to have to go with another white tee and will probably just have to forgo the button-down. I don't think I have another that's close enough. I should really just start buying things in doubles for instances like this."

I laughed because I had thought the exact same thing once upon a time. "Gleaming white T-shirt it is, but I will grab you another shirt that is at least close in case it gets chilly. With night vision, maybe it won't be noticeable. Or we can explain it away on camera some-how. Do you need jeans?"

"It flew, didn't drop, thank goodness. I was able to clean off the couple of spots on my lower half. My torso is a lost cause. Ah, crap. I gotta run. We have another rush, and I'm short-staffed. See you soon?"

"Absolutely. I'll be there as soon as I can." I disconnected.

I'd always found it admirable that Pax had started and ran a soup kitchen in the neighborhood. Even with as busy as he was, he still found a way to put in time there himself. He'd hired a great staff to oversee things when he had to work the show, but he always made sure to make an appearance and offer counseling and support, and nearly every extra dime he made went into Chasing Hope. He even had about six cots in a new build section of the warehouse and used it as a shelter for when things got really bad with some of his regulars, or he saw people in need on the streets. We'd talked in great detail about how it bothered him that he couldn't help everyone, but he had a soft spot for women and children and did everything he could to ensure they were safe and on the right path to rehabil-itation.

I didn't know a ton about Pax's past—he was pretty tight-lipped about it—but in the years I'd known him, I'd learned enough and read between the lines enough times to know that he had a very strained relationship with his father. His mother had died some time ago of cancer, right about the time Pax had lost his collar and his grandfather disappeared I believed, and his dad and sister had basically cut him off. I didn't know if it had to do with what'd happened with Pax and the Church or what, seeing as Pax's father was also a priest, and a very well-established one at that. He'd apparently even been given special permission by the bishop to perform major rites of exorcism and was always a backup if we ever needed some big guns on the show despite their estrangement. He was the only exorcist in the area, after all. Still, it always seemed to me that Pax was searching for a way to fill a void in his life. To do even more good than he already did. And I wasn't entirely sure why. Maybe I'd ask him one of these days.

I pulled up to Pax's house and shut off the engine, getting out of the car and eyeing what looked to be about three steps from the porch. Just as Pax had said, one of the pavers was a bit more orange than the rest and it came up easily, revealing a weatherproof box and the spare key inside.

I let myself into the home and took in the interior. I had been to Pax's house several times before to pick him up or drop him off but had never been inside. It surprised me a little. I wasn't sure why, but I'd expected the quintessential bachelor pad. What I found was a cozy home with mismatched furniture that somehow still all worked together, and accents that were purposeful and not haphazard. He even had accent pillows; something most guys I'd met insisted were pointless and stupid. I smiled and nodded, thinking I'd have to tell him that I approved.

I made my way through the house to where I assumed the master bedroom was. As I walked down the hall, I stopped to take in the gallery of framed photographs, seeing Pax at different ages with different people. He honestly hadn't changed much. And he always looked carefree and happy. There was one of him on a mountain—I'd had no idea he was the adventurous sort. Another of him with who I assumed was his younger sister on a beach. There was one of him in his clerical gear with a few other priests outside of what looked to be a monastery, somewhere exotic. Maybe even Tibet.

When I got to the end of the hall, the largest picture pulled me in. It was of a much younger Paxton, maybe in his early twenties, in front of a large house, his arm around an older man who looked so much like Pax, I knew they were related. But the age difference was much greater than father and son. I assumed it was his grandfather. The man had on black clothing, his priest's collar gleaming in contrast. Pax was dressed casually as he always was, but the love on his face was evident for all to see.

I moved in closer and took in the other man's features. He looked so familiar to me, though I wasn't sure why. Maybe it was just the resemblance. After all, I spent a lot of time taking Pax in when he wasn't looking. Seriously, the guy was hot. Like h-a-w-t hot. But it felt like it was more than that. Maybe I'd seen him around town. New Orleans was big, but it wasn't all that big, and the world tended to be a much smaller place than most people realized.

I shook myself out of my reverie and made my way to the room at the end of the hall, entering a bedroom done in rich wood with dark blues and soft greens and accents of, interestingly enough, peach. It was warm and inviting and kind of sexy, and I once again gave Pax props for his decorating style.

I found another bright white T-shirt in the dresser, grabbed a flannel from the walk-in, and made my way back out to the car, locking up behind myself and securing the key back where I'd found it.

When I reached the soup kitchen, I saw the line out the door. I checked my watch and noticed that we only had an hour and a half before we needed to be back at Lamour. I grabbed an energy shot out of my bag, downed it in a gulp, and headed inside with Pax's clothes.

He saw me as I walked in and waved me over from behind the counter. He looked adorable in his apron and hair net, but I saw that his shirt was, indeed, an absolute mess. He hadn't been kidding.

"Hey," I said as I reached him. "Hopping place today."

He rolled his eyes. "Understatement of the year. And one of my newest hires up and quit this morning with no notice, so when I got here, the rest of them were trying to hold down the fort without bothering me but it was clear they were struggling. I had to jump in and help. What time is it?"

I looked at my watch again. "Too late for you to still be this busy. Do you want some help?"

He stared at me for a beat. "Are you serious?"

"As a heart attack. Just give me an apron and one of those fancy hats, and I'll slop some grub."

"Damn, woman. I could kiss you," he said and turned away to go and grab me what I needed. At least, I assumed. But that wasn't what had my attention. What did was the way my insides reacted when he'd said what he had. My libido perked up as if saying, *Yes, please*.

When he came back, my gaze immediately went to his mouth. His full, plump lips the color of sugared strawberries. I wondered if they'd taste as sweet as they looked.

I reached back, pulling my hair into a messy bun at the nape of my neck and securing it with the hair tie I always kept around my wrist before looking up. His eyes were chips of ice, but they weren't cold. No, they burned. His gaze rose from my chest and clashed with mine, and I saw the interest there. Interest I knew was mirrored on my face.

He handed me a bundle, and I got to work donning my gear before taking the spot beside him to help dish stew to the queue of patrons.

An hour later, everyone had been served, he'd recruited some regulars to help clean up by offering them some money for their next evening meal outside of the kitchen, instructed his staff to keep an eye on things and take care of the restaurant vouchers, and we were cleaned up and ready to head back to the Lamour Mansion.

"Thank you for stepping in today," he said and straightened the tails of the shirt I'd brought for him.

"My pleasure," I said and let my hair down, shaking out the long, thick strands with my hands and giving my scalp a rest since I figured I'd probably have it up for most of the night. "You looked like you could use it, and it weirdly invigorated me. I was feeling super drained, but just being in here with you gave me a boost."

He smiled and handed me a bottle of water. "As exhausting as it can be, I completely understand what you mean. I think it's the Karma."

I laughed. "It's interesting to hear you talk about Karma, *Padre*." I grinned and took a sip of the water.

He hitched a thumb at himself. "Not a one-trick pony. JC may be my homeboy, but I'm a well-rounded spiritual gangsta."

I lost it and sprayed my mouthful of water all over

the place. Choking, I tried to get the words out. "Wow. Okay. Props for originality." I winked. "What do you say we skedaddle?"

"Yeah, we'd better get. I'm sure Dev is champing at the bit to do our day two catch-up before we get going again. After you," he said and gestured towards the door.

I walked in front of him, putting a little extra swing in my hips for good measure.

I mean . . . why not?

CHAPTER 10

~Paxton~

The woman would be the death of me. I couldn't stop thinking about her. And working with her so closely lately wasn't helping. The only thing that didn't make me feel like a lecher was that I saw how she looked at me. There was definite interest there. I suspected that if I asked her out, she'd probably say yes. But that was the last thing we needed right now. At least during an investigation of this magnitude. Maybe after we'd wrapped things up at Lamour.

Maybe.

Sky and I parked in front of the house and made our way inside, seeing that things were buzzing. Like every day right before a shoot, prep was in full swing.

We'd settle in in a bit to get the latest from everybody and go over shooting assignments, but at this point, it was all checking and double-checking equipment and batteries, re-evaluating camera positioning and cable connectivity, and other necessary but inane things. With a twenty-thousand-square-foot location, not to mention the area outside we'd set aside to investigate if we had time, it was a big task.

"Where do you want us?" I asked the room at large when we walked in. Dev looked up from what he'd been doing near the desk with Turner and smiled.

"Hey, guys," he said. "How was the kitchen, Padre?"

"Crazy-busy," I answered. "Thank goodness Sky saved me by bringing new clothes and offered to help for the last rush."

"Good on you," Hanlen said as she walked into the room, offering a fist for Sky to bump. "Everything's set in the attic, babe," she said to Dev. "You guys can check the camera output."

I looked at Hanlen. "You put static cameras in the attic?"

"Yeah," she said. "After what happened yesterday, we didn't really want you guys up there without some extra eyes and ears."

I nodded and saw Sky doing the same.

"So, I take it that's where you want us?" Sky said.

"If you're up for it." Dev wrapped a cable around his hand and elbow, making a loop.

Sky looked at me, and I shrugged. "Why not?"

"Yeah, okay," she said and went to check her gear.

I walked over to the table to see that they'd added another monitor that had a quad-box. It looked like they had a new camera in the attic, one more in the landing hallway between the second and third floors, and one outside focused on the big live oak in the yard.

"What monitoring devices do we get tonight?" I asked.

Van came over. "Dev wants to try out the JumpBox tonight. We figured you could take the Geoport, and Lark will use the Wonder Box. You guys should all get the same results as you did with the JumpBox since they all basically do the same thing, just with slightly different technologies. You just won't get the visual output of the words."

"Works for me," I said. They were all great devices, but I loved using the new stuff that Lennie and Van came up with. They were always making the equipment we already loved better, and it was fun to see what they could come up with next. I hoped they found a way to make what they did even more profitable. I knew they were looking into a side endeavor on a nearby island. It'd be interesting to see if anything came of it.

The sun sank into the horizon, casting the mansion in shadows. It felt even more ominous tonight than it had the night before and I was curious to see what might shake out as the investigation progressed.

Birdie came into the room, and I took in her face. She looked a little drawn. "Hey," I called. "You okay?"

She moved closer to me. "Yeah. I just don't like the

way things feel in here tonight. It's like balancing on the edge of a rooftop, you know? Either you're gonna fall, or someone's going to pull you back to safety."

"I was just thinking the same. It feels more charged in here tonight. And not in a good way."

"No, definitely not good," Dakota said as she joined us and rubbed at her temple.

"All right, guys," Dev said and looked around the room. "As I'm sure any of you with any sensitivities have already figured, things are more active tonight. Our ghost crew checked in earlier and said we need to be extra aware. They said that things have really gotten shaken up for some reason—more than we usually encounter after we inevitably stir things. They counted no less than fourteen different presences earlier, and they think there are more. They also said that what we assume is the malevolent entity, likely the non-human one, is extra amped tonight. We assumed that us poking around last night would probably provoke things—and it did, which is why we cut early—but . . . just look alive. Be aware, protect yourselves, and keep in contact at all times."

"I'd like to do a blessing if everyone's okay with it," Birdie said, and everyone nodded. Even Sky.

"Please join hands." We all did, and she bowed her head. "Lord and Lady, working for me and through me, thank you for your blessings on this day and every day. I ask that you watch over this group as we undertake our work for the night. Dearly departed, angels, ancestors, and guides, lead us in our endeavors and shield us from evil. Hold us in your light and warn us of danger as we shall watch out for you. By the Divine power of three times three, this is my will, so mote it be."

I said another quick mental prayer of protection and whispered a quick, "Amen," and we all dropped hands.

It was time to get to work.

Sky and I were taking Aaron with us tonight up into the attic. I glanced at the younger man and saw him pound the last of his energy drink and crack his knuckles. I wasn't sure how he hadn't had a heart attack yet with as much caffeine and sugar as he knocked back on a daily basis, but I figured it probably helped that he spent every free waking moment in the gym. The guy was huge. But he was a giant teddy bear and great at his job, and we were lucky to have him.

"Ready to rock, kids?" he asked, and I grinned. He called everybody *kid* regardless of how senior they were.

Sky finished securing her hair in a bun and stuck her pen in it, then grabbed her Handycam and handed me the Geoport. "Ready, Freddie."

"All right, let's do this," I said and looked around, watching the rest of the cast and crew breaking off into their respective groups to go and tackle the areas they had been assigned.

I had a ball of lead in my stomach. For some reason, the idea of going into the attic made me super uneasy. I wasn't sure why, but I knew I needed to be on my toes tonight. We headed up the left side of the staircase, having taken the right side last time, and then rounded the landing where the two sides met and took the hall to the door that led to the third-floor stairwell. Like last night, the area felt electrified, and we all said as much and documented what we could before heading up to the third level.

Dev wanted us to do a quick sweep of the other larger bedroom on the third floor tonight before going the rest of the way up to the attic, and I almost felt relieved that we had a bit of a delay from the inevitable. Something about even the idea of that space made me uneasy.

We entered the room, and I took a seat on the bed to get the Geoport set up, setting my walkie on the side table as Aaron and Sky got some shots of the room with their cameras. I heard Sky in the large bathroom, doing a quick recording session for EVP with her normal mini-recorder, and then both she and Aaron came back out.

"Okay, let's see if anybody feels like chatting," I said and fired up the Geoport. "Is anybody in here with us?" I asked.

The device bleeped and blarted, the white noise echoing through the speakers a bit as it scanned its radio frequencies, but we didn't get any intelligent feedback. At least, not yet.

"Lillian, are you here?" I asked, wondering if the starlet was around tonight.

"What were the missing homeowners' names?" Aaron asked, and I tried to remember.

"Um . . ." Sky said. "I think the first one's name was Craig. The second Brittany. And . . ."

"Edward," I said, remembering the name of the last missing homeowner.

"*Ed.*" Came a voice from the Geoport.

I raised a brow and glanced at Sky. She shrugged and gestured for me to continue. "Edward, is that you?" I asked.

"*Dead.*"

"Why do I feel like we should be doing that children's rhyme? This is Fred. Fred is dead," Aaron asked, and Sky and I laughed.

"We're sorry that happened to you," I said and waited to see if we'd get more. When we didn't, I continued. "Do you remember what happened?"

"*Taken.*"

"Who took you?" I asked. I wondered if maybe we could find out that he had been kidnapped by a person and not stolen away by a demon. How cool would that be if we could help solve a cold case? Sky would be over the moon.

"*Evil.*"

Well, that could go either way. People were sometimes the worst kinds of monsters.

Another voice came through the box. "*Where's the child?*"

We didn't always get complete sentences, especially with the Geoport. That was interesting. And it meant that we were dealing with a strong and intelligent presence.

"Who are you? What's your name?" I asked, hoping to get an identity for the new voice.

"*Attic.*"

"Good grief. I can't believe I'm asking this . . . You want us to go to the attic?" Sky said.

"*Yes.*"

"Well, lucky for you, we were already headed there," Aaron chimed in. "What do you think, kids? Should we head on up?"

"Now's as good a time as any, I suppose."

We were headed down the hall towards the door that led to the attic when I heard something. I stopped. "Did you guys hear that?" I asked.

"Some kind of knocking, right?" Sky said.

"I heard it, too," Aaron confirmed.

"It sounded like it did last night. Three quick raps. But I couldn't tell where they came from. Could you?" I looked at Sky.

The knocking came again. Three more taps in quick succession.

"If I had to guess," she said, "I'd say from above, but it's hard to tell with how this place echoes, and we don't know what's up there that could be causing it."

"What the hell was that?" Aaron suddenly said, and Sky and I turned to see him spinning to face the other direction.

"What?"

"I swear I just saw something walking down the hall."

"Where? Could it have been someone from the cast?" Sky asked.

"Down there. Towards the end of the hall. It was like a black mass. Kind of human-shaped but not really."

"Did you catch it on camera?" I inquired.

"It was slightly in my peripheral vision, but my body was partly turned that way. I hope so. The camera should have a wide enough angle on the lens," he said.

"Oh, shit." I shook my head.

"What?" Sky moved closer.

"I left the walkie in the bedroom. Give me a second to grab it before we head up."

She and Aaron nodded, and I turned and clicked on my mini-flashlight, ready to head back to the bedroom. Suddenly, I stopped, something grabbing my attention out of the corner of my eye. I crouched and shone the light on the floor, noticing the moisture there. I moved the beam up the hall a ways and saw that there was more.

"Uh, guys?"

They both came up to me, and I hit the puddles with the light. "You're seeing this, right?"

"What the hell?" Seemed it would be a repetitive statement for Aaron tonight.

Sky crouched beside me and took in what I was looking at. She reached out and swiped her finger through it before I could stop her.

"Sky!" I exclaimed.

"What?" she said. "We need to see what it is." She brought her finger to her nose and sniffed.

"If you put that in your mouth," Aaron said, "I'm quitting. Probably after I puke all over you. Just don't."

She rolled her eyes and shot him a glare. "It's water, you big baby. But where did it come from?" She looked at the walls and the ceiling, felt the floor beyond and in front of the areas affected and then shook her head.

I had no idea. But . . . "There have been documented cases of demonic hauntings where unexplained moisture became present. Footsteps of water with no feet to leave them. Oil seeping from plastic window blinds with no explanation. Cabinets dripping with no rhyme or reason and not from anyplace that could cause it. Make sure to get this all on film. I'll be right back."

I took a few more steps towards the bedroom we had been in earlier when the other three bedroom doors and the bathroom door suddenly slammed closed.

"The fuck?" Aaron exclaimed and jumped, spinning to face the other end of the hall.

"Here we go again," I mumbled. "Aaron, watch her for a second. I'll be quick." I jogged into the room, swiped up the walkie, and ran back out, narrowly missing getting my hand broken as I grabbed the jamb to round the corner just as that door slammed shut, too.

"*That* was close," I said and turned to look at the now-closed slab of wood.

"Are you okay?" Sky called.

"Fine. But what do you say we get out of here?"

"Uh, yeah. I'm all for that," Aaron said and raised the hand not balancing the camera.

I palmed the scapular on the back of my neck and mumbled a prayer as I followed Sky and Aaron down the hall. Something wasn't right here. Sky opened the door to the attic stairs and started up a few steps before turning back to us. "Do you think we should do a Geoport and EMF session here before we head up? Dev would probably appreciate that," she said.

"Good idea." I squatted, turning the Geoport on and getting it ready, assuming that Sky was using the K2 meter on the stairs, when I heard Aaron grunt.

"Ow. Fucking hell. That burns."

"Whaa—?" I started, barely lifting my head, when I saw him holding up his arm into the light from the camera and peering down at it. Just as I was about to move closer with the flashlight to take a look for myself, I heard a blood-curdling scream. I lifted my head and saw Sky being dragged up the stairs by nothing, her arms flailing, and her feet scissoring, the sounds coming out of her mouth dumping electricity into my veins.

"SKY!" I yelled, rushing after her, only to have the stairwell door slam in my face before I could reach it. I hit the floor, the air forced out of my lungs with an *oof*, but bounced right back up and returned to the door. I pounded on it, pulled on the handle with all my might, trying to get it to budge—to no avail.

Aaron set down the camera and came to help me,

and even with two of us, we couldn't get the door to open. I still heard Sky screaming from upstairs, and my stomach turned. I wanted to vomit, but we honestly didn't have time for that. We needed to get to her. Now. Just as I was racking my brain, trying to think of something we could use to get the door open, the Geoport squawked.

"*Mine.*"

"Fuck," Aaron and I said in unison and resumed our efforts to get into the stairwell.

CHAPTER 11

~Schuyler~

Something I couldn't see yanked me up the stairs and threw me across the floor. I slid several feet until I hit the wall on the far side of the room, headfirst, a cloud of dust pluming, making my eyes water and my sinuses seize.

"Fuck."

I coughed and took quick stock of my body, making sure that nothing was broken. I was definitely bruised, probably had a concussion now, and my heart felt as if it might beat out of my chest, but I was okay for the most part. Physically, anyway. Mentally, I felt a bit . . . shattered.

What the actual fuck just happened?

The doors closing and seeming to lock both

yesterday and earlier, while unusual, *could* still be explained. These old houses had weird drafts. If one door opened, it could cause updrafts that created vacuums. Wood warped. Old locks had a tendency to latch and then pop loose with enough rattling. Hell, my *brand-new* door lock at home routinely locked me out if it was just a little bit turned and I didn't notice before I shut the door behind me. Being dragged up an entire set of stairs by something that had no form and thrown across the room utterly defied explanation. And working for a paranormal reality show, we had all been taught that if it had no explanation, it was likely supernatural, or as I'd heard Pax refer to it before—a negative miracle.

Just as I was about to sit up and then try to stand, I felt a force come down over me, pressing me against the floor and restricting my movements. I felt invisible hands wrap around my throat and cut off my airflow. I thrashed and fought, clawing at my neck and kicking my feet, trying to get purchase enough to get out from whatever held me down, but I couldn't break free.

An insidious voice whispered in my head, and horrible images flashed. The voice told me that I was theirs. That I should have always been theirs. That my soul belonged to them. That I had been promised, and they would take. The images showed those same cloaked figures I'd dreamt about. That same male with the dagger and chalice. But this time, I saw a beast, too. Easily seven feet tall and horned like a bull, with eyes like dark pits, claws of flame, and what appeared to be scales on bits of its skin.

No. I refused to die this way. No fucking way would I let this be my end. I didn't even really believe in this shit. I remembered something that Dev had taught us early on. Something he used to remind us about before every show when the series first started. And I could get on board with the whole mind-over-matter thing.

"You are not allowed to hurt me!" I choked out as loudly as I could and coughed, able to wheeze in half a breath. "You don't have permission to touch me. I do not allow you to interact with me in this world."

Just as quickly as the weight had settled on me, I heard a groaned, *"Nooo,"* in my head, and the force disappeared. I rolled onto my side, propped on an elbow, and sucked in air, coughing and willing my vision to return to normal, and for the dots filling it to leave. The entire space smelled of ozone, and I couldn't control the roiling of my stomach. I threw up everything I'd had earlier. Just as I flopped onto my back and covered my face with my hands, I heard the door at the bottom of the stairwell hit the wall with a crash and crack, followed by thundering footsteps ascending the stairs.

Before I could even take another breath, someone pulled me forward and to the side, hauled me into a lap, and cradled me against a chest that smelled of Hugo Boss. Then, I heard another voice.

"9-1-1, yo. We need everybody—and I do mean *everybody*—up in the attic. Pronto," Aaron said.

"What's going on?" I heard Dev say through the walkie.

"What about *pronto* and 9-1-1 did you not understand, bro? Just get your asses up here. Now. Fucking hell."

"On our way."

I felt a hand on my calf. "Jesus fucking Christ, Sky—uh, sorry, Padre—but, really. Holy shit. Are you okay? That was . . . I don't even have words."

I lowered my hands and looked at Aaron. "For the most part, yeah, I'm okay. At least, I think." I looked at him closer and noticed that he was bleeding. "What happened to you?"

"Just as you were nabbed, I got scratched. Bad. I think it could have been a distraction. We were focused on that right when you were yanked, and the door slammed shut."

He had three deep gashes in his forearm, each of them still welling blood. "You need to get that looked at. If you ran into something, you could get tetanus."

He laughed. "Sky, girl, you just got hauled up the stairs by your hair by a freaking demon or some shit, and you're worried about these cat scratches on me? Let's tackle these crises in order of importance, 'kay?"

I chuckled and then groaned when my head protested. Pax adjusted his hold but didn't let me go. He still hadn't said anything, though. I shifted so I could turn and see his face. He was paler than I had ever seen anybody, and I felt the trembling in his body as he cradled me. He had his eyes closed, and his lips were moving, but he wasn't saying anything out loud. I assumed he was praying, and at this point, and after what'd just happened, I didn't even care.

I reached up and touched his cheek, and he opened his eyes. I saw tears in his baby blues and felt my heart clench. Aside from my parents, I wasn't sure that anyone had ever shown such concern for me before.

"I'm okay," I said.

He lowered his gaze to my neck and gently brushed his fingers across my throat. I felt it then. The tenderness and pain. I could almost feel the tissue swelling.

He shook his head and then closed his eyes again, taking in a deep breath. His entire body was a ball of tension. If there had been something in front of us for him to take his anger out on, I didn't think they'd stand a chance. Pacifist or no, I had a feeling that Pax was ready to kill for me. And while it shouldn't, that warmed something inside me.

I heard footsteps on the stairs and looked over to see Dev, Hanlen, Lark, and several other members of the cast and crew filing into the room.

"What's going on?" Dev said, his eyes widening when he saw me and Pax on the side of the room and the path in the dust my body had created, and then noticed Aaron's bloody arm. "*Merde*. Seems we really did miss some things. Are you guys okay? What the hell happened?"

Pax just looked at Dev and shook his head, seemingly not able to find the words. Dev looked at me then.

"I'm not sure," I said honestly, my voice cracking. "We investigated the other bedroom as you asked. Pax thinks we may have made contact with Edward, one of the missing homeowners. The voice told us his name was Ed and that he'd been taken—"

"By evil," Aaron finished.

I shot him a glare. "We got the words *taken* and *evil* on the Geoport, take that however you will. Anyway, another voice came through after and we actually got a full sentence." I paused. "It said, '*Where's the child?*'"

"Where's the child?" Hanlen said. "Didn't you guys get something yesterday about a mother?"

I had totally forgotten about that. We had. Along with the *apple* EVP. "We left the room and were about to make our way to the attic when Pax noticed moisture in a trail on the hallway floor. There wasn't any logical explanation for it that we could find. We also heard knocking a few times. In threes. But we couldn't figure out where, exactly, the sound was coming from."

Pax tightened his hold around me briefly, and it centered me a little. I figured it might be doing the same for him, so I stayed right where I was. "Pax had forgotten his walkie in the bedroom, so he went to get it. Suddenly, all the doors in the hall slammed closed. I thought maybe it was some sort of updraft and vacuum or something. We decided to get out of there and continue on, and I started up. A few steps in, I figured maybe we should do a Geoport session quick before we headed up. As we were getting ready to do that, I heard Aaron say something and then something grabbed and yanked me—up the damn stairs. I fought as hard as I could, but I couldn't get away."

Aaron scrubbed a hand through his hair. "She's right. I did say something. I said 'ow.' And I'm sure I probably swore a blue streak. It burned like a bitch. But as Padre and I were checking out my arm, we heard Sky scream and looked up to see her being shuttled up the steps. We barely took a step forward to help when that last door slammed closed and locked on us."

Dev looked haunted. I meant no pun by the thought, but the descriptor of the expression sort of fit. "Like yesterday. I don't like this, guys." He looked at Birdie, and I saw her standing with wide eyes and her hand over her mouth.

She shook her head. "I told you I had a bad feeling about the energy in this place from the first time I stepped foot in here. Not all of it is bad, as we've found throughout the investigation so far, but most of it is. And given what Dakota and I have experienced psychically, I can say with definitive sureness that this is nothing human. We're not dealing with a residual haunting or poltergeist activity here. This is demonic. And we're all in danger."

She looked at me. "How are you feeling, Sky?"

"My body hurts. I have a hell of a headache from being thrown into the wall and trying to figure out what the fuck could have caused this, and my throat is getting more and more sore from being choked."

"Wait, what?" Dev asked.

I blew air out of my nose. "I didn't finish the story.

So, after I was yanked up the steps, whatever it was tossed me like a bag of feed. I flew across the floor,"—I pointed to the track in the dust and dirt—"and slid, only stopping when the top of my head hit the wall behind me."

"Jesus," James said.

"Oh, it gets worse," I added. "I took stock of how I was feeling and was about to get up when something came down on top of me. I couldn't move at all really. Was able to kick my feet a bit but that was about it. And then it choked me. I got my hands up, but it didn't do any good. And I got all sorts of awful . . . things in my head."

"What kinds of things?" Dev asked.

"I think it wants me for some reason. Or I'm losing it. Probably losing it. It said it would have me. I saw images of what appeared to be some sort of ritual going on, but it was all things I'd seen in my nightmares lately, so it could have just been lack of oxygen to the brain." I noticed Birdie and Dev share a look. "But then I remembered what you taught us, boss." I looked at him. "I told it that it didn't have permission to affect me, and it let me go."

Dev ran a hand down his face. "You've been having weird dreams?" he asked, and I nodded.

"When did they start?"

"Umm . . ." I said, "we were still investigating Arborwood."

"Right after you came out here the first time?" Birdie asked.

I thought back. "Yeah, I think it was, actually. But I haven't been feeling all that well, either. I've been really tired, and my moods have been all over the place. I was actually thinking I should talk to Harper and go and see my primary."

"Oh, Sky," Dakota said and turned away from me, and I felt Padre's hold tighten even more.

"What?" I asked, looking from person to person in the room.

Dev ran an agitated hand through his hair. "All of that equals signs of oppression, Sky. Once a place is infested, the malignant entity moves on to oppression, both with the place and the people who come into contact with it. It'll step up its game with physical attacks, sleep disturbances, anxiety and depression, bad luck, troubles at work and at home . . . all sorts of stuff. We need to get to the bottom of what's going on here. Immediately." He looked at Birdie and then at Dakota.

"Have you two received anything? Any messages from spirit that could help?" They shook their heads.

"I haven't gotten anything, either, but my abilities don't really work that way. However, I just realized that I haven't seen Wren, Findley, Gunnie, or Desmond tonight. That's unusual. I wonder if something's keeping them out of the house."

"You know, I didn't even register that, boss," Birdie said. "I usually get occasional commentary from them during an investigation, too,"—she tapped her temple—"and I haven't heard a peep."

"I don't feel safe," Dakota said, her voice smaller and quieter than I'd ever heard it.

"I'm not sure any of us should feel safe." Dev looked at her, reaching out to squeeze her shoulder before pulling Hanlen to him and checking his watch. "It's two a.m. I don't think we should stay through the witching hour."

"Fucking Devil's hour, more like it," Aaron said, and most everyone nodded.

"Padre, I think you should take Sky to the emergency room to get checked out. Are you okay to do that?"

I felt Pax move behind me and assumed he'd nodded. I didn't like how quiet he was.

"Everybody else, let's wrap things up as much as we can in the next half hour, get as much as we can for the final show—I hate to even say that given what's going on, but until I can talk to the network, Roch, and the owners, we are still on a timetable—and then get out of here. Aaron, clean up that arm. And use some holy water before you take care of it medically. We need to do some more digging into what might be going on, and I think that Lark and I should perform some rituals in the morning to negate some of this shit."

Birdie looked at him, a very serious expression on her face. "We might make it worse, Dev."

He twisted his lips. "Yeah, we might. But right now, I can't decide what's the lesser of the two evils there. Trying and *maybe* helping with the realization that we could be provoking it; or leaving it alone and letting it get stronger naturally." He looked around the room. "Let's get to it, guys. Sky, are you okay to walk?"

"Yeah," I said and tried to pull away from Pax. He wouldn't let me go. I turned in his hold again and looked at him. He still appeared in shock, so I put a palm on his cheek again, and he seemed to snap out of it a little. "You need to let me go, Pax. Dev is right. I should probably go to the hospital and get looked over. I don't feel too horrible, but better safe than sorry, right?"

"Okay." That was all he said as he moved and helped me to stand, supporting me the entire time. It wasn't much, but it was something, and given the hellish— literally—events of the night, stuff that my mind couldn't compute and put into its usual orderly columns, I'd take any win I could get. But it concerned me greatly that I didn't feel like myself at all. Just thinking that any of this *could* be explained somehow, or that it was okay that it *couldn't* be, should have been a red flag for me.

CHAPTER 12

~Paxton~

I drove in silence, sneaking peeks at Sky from the corner of my eye. She had an elbow resting on the armrest of the door, her head in her hand, and her eyes closed. I still couldn't believe what'd happened tonight. Replayed visions of seeing her dragged up the stairs, and stills of her lying on the floor with those purple marks around her neck would haunt me forever. I wasn't entirely sure what we'd tell the hospital. She looked as if she'd been abused. And she had, but not by a domestic partner. Not by anything that could be easily explained to medical personnel. Generally, physical marks inflicted by something not of this world faded quickly, but it wouldn't be quick enough for the ER.

I refocused on the road and got us to University Medical Center safely. Helping her out of the truck and supporting her, I noticed that the parking lot wasn't too full. It was the wee hours of the morning, but that was usually a hopping time for New Orleans. Bourbon Street didn't seem to sleep, and it sometimes felt like the full moons lasted all month.

We got into the emergency department, and I had her take a seat as I took her ID and insurance card and went to check her in. Less than a half an hour later, we were in triage, and they were doing vitals, putting in an IV just in case, taking blood, and doing all the things. We'd lucked out, and I knew the nurse assigned to her case. Jane was actually married to my good friend, Jeffrey, and knew what we did for a living. When I explained to her what'd happened, she'd just nodded and made appropriate notes on the chart, assuring me that she'd assign us to a doctor who would understand, as well. I was sure we'd probably still have to answer a bunch of extra questions, and may get a visit from a hospital caseworker in addition to the normal medical personnel, but we'd at least avoided major drama upfront.

They got us into a private cubicle and took Sky off for x-rays and scans. I could only sit there with my head hung, thinking of how close things had gotten tonight. And we weren't out of the woods yet. This thing had a foothold and it wanted Sky for reasons still unknown. It baffled me. She wasn't the most vulnerable of the group. Yes, she was susceptible in a way because she didn't believe, but that could go either way. These things fed off acknowledgment. If a person didn't believe that they existed, it threatened the entity, and they lost some of their power. In the same token, however, if you didn't know what to look out for, you couldn't protect yourself from it, and a strong enough evil could use that to gain ground.

One thing I knew for certain, I wasn't letting her out of my sight. She'd probably balk and argue, but either she was staying at my place—which was preferred since I knew my house was blessed—or I was bunking on her couch. There would be no compromise. One or the other. Or I was taking her to Arborwood and having Hanlen and Dev lock her in one of their guest suites as Birdie spelled the door.

The nurse wheeled Sky back into the room, and I took her in. She looked beat but seemed alert. Once she was again reclined on the bed, I reached over and took her hand.

"How are you holding up?"

She looked at me, her dark eyes bottomless. I could get lost in them, and I found myself thinking how I couldn't even imagine never being able to look into them again. "I'm okay, actually. They gave me some anti-inflammatory meds and they must have kicked in because I feel better than I did before for sure. They said the x-rays were normal. We're just waiting on the scans. If there's no bleeding or anything in the results, they told me I could go home."

"About that," I started. "I don't want you to be alone, Sky."

She squeezed my hand. "I'm fine. Really."

"I know that. I know you are now. Right now. But you weren't, and I don't think you're going to be. Here's the thing. I know you don't really believe in all of this stuff beyond what you can scientifically explain away. All of that remains in that grey area of your brain that you can't necessarily ignore but don't put too much stock in. But you can't deny what happened tonight. There's absolutely no scientific explanation for it. And what happened was a demoniacal attack."

She bit her lip and then shrugged a shoulder. "Okay, yeah. I can't find anything to explain it, but that doesn't mean I'm ready to praise god for saving me."

"Sky . . ." I warned.

"No disrespect intended, Pax. Not really. Okay, maybe a little. But I'm still an atheist. That hasn't changed in the last handful of hours."

"A priest friend of mine once said that you'll never find an atheist in a haunted house." She smiled as I intended, and I returned the grin. "But, Sky, there are two sides to that coin. You can't deny what happened tonight. You may not want to put into words what that was, but I'll do it for you. You were physically affected by a negative diabolical intelligence. And once they get a foothold, it doesn't stop until they get what they came for."

"What's that?" she said and snorted. "My soul?" Her voice dripped with derision.

"Yes."

She laughed. "Okay, *Padre*. I don't want to argue with you. I'm just too damn tired. Can we just agree that there was some really whacky energy tonight? I'm fine. Honest."

I shook my head. "You're not. And your extra snark proves it." I pulled my hand away from hers and scrubbed it through my hair. "But all of that aside, until we know more and can narrow down what might be going on in that house, I would feel better if you weren't alone. You probably shouldn't be alone anyway given the injuries, even if they do clear you to leave the hospital."

She sighed. "Okay, listen. I'm too damn tired to argue with you, and it's a stupid thing to argue about anyway. You can sleep on my couch. It kind of sucks, but you can."

I looked at her, hoping she'd agree to this. "How would you feel about staying at my place? I have a comfortable spare." I hoped this next little bit might convince her. She was a woman of logic, after all. "And it's closer to Lamour."

"Okay, all right, I see what you did there, you sneaky bastard. Playing to my sense of logic. Fine. But only because I really like your house. I didn't know you were such a good decorator. Should I start calling you Martha Stewart?"

That made me smile. "You like my house?"

"I do," she said. "When I went to get your clothes, I was super impressed. I love the colors you chose, and it's so homey. And extra points for not having creepy crucifixes hanging and sitting on every flat surface."

Something inside me warmed at the thought of her liking my haven. And the holy objects were there, they just weren't overt. It was one of the reasons I really wanted her in my place. We would be protected there more than we would be in other places. But if I were honest, it was only one of the reasons I wanted her in my space. The thought of her among my stuff made me feel things I wasn't sure I wanted to think more about quite yet.

The nurse came in then, a big smile on her face. "Ms. Liu, I have excellent news. The doctor said that the scans were all clean. You are free to leave. I'll start drawing up the paperwork now. But she said she would like you to have someone with you tonight just in case. Is that possible?" She looked at me, and I turned to Sky.

"We were actually just talking about that," Sky said. "It's covered."

"Excellent," the nurse replied. "I'll be back right quick with your discharge papers to sign. Here's the other paperwork for your visit with us tonight. Blood work numbers, scan and x-ray results, diagnoses and recommendations. You know, the usual." She handed a bunch of papers to Sky and hurried from the room.

Sky leafed through the stack quickly and then flipped back to the beginning, suddenly becoming still.

"What is it?" I asked. "Did they miss something?"

With her science background, she could likely understand it all. "Do we need to call her back?"

"No, it's . . ." Her brow furrowed. "I don't think I've ever seen my blood type on paperwork before. I know that's weird, but I don't think I have. And I'm not sure I remembered what it was, either."

"Okay. *Why* is that important?"

"Because with the stuff that Mom and Dad went through with that major car accident they were in a few years ago, I know *their* blood types. Dad is A+ and Mom is O+."

"*And?*" I prompted.

"I'm B-. That's not possible, Pax." She looked at me. "Not if they're my parents."

CHAPTER 13

~Schuyler~

*W*e pulled into Paxton's driveway after stopping off at my place for some stuff, and Pax put the truck in park before helping me out of the vehicle and up the steps of his porch. I felt okay, but he was still treating me as if I were made of spun glass. The girly part of me enjoyed it, though, so I wasn't about to say anything. At least, not unless or until he did something that crossed the line between chivalry and being overbearing. But I couldn't see him doing that.

He led me through the house to the spare bedroom across the hall and a bit down from the master and set my stuff on the bed, showing me where the towels were and all the things I'd need.

"Are you hungry?" he asked.

Surprisingly, I was, despite everything that'd happened and the stew of confusion going on in my head. "Yeah, I could eat. Are we ordering in?"

"Nah. I thought I'd make us something. Is there anything you won't or can't eat?"

"Wait, you cook?"

He smiled. "I run a soup kitchen. Did you really think I couldn't cook?"

I shrugged. "I'm . . . sorry? For some reason, in the back of my mind, I just didn't see you as the domestic type. After seeing your place earlier, though, I should have figured. Are you like a chef-level cook, or just a passable cook? Should I look into booking you a spot on *Top Chef*?"

He shook his head, a smile flirting with his lips. "How does a western omelet and homemade biscuits sound? And not the ones from a can or eggs with frozen veggies. The real deal."

"Damn. You may have just found a way to my heart. Especially since I can't cook worth shit."

He chuckled, shook his head, and gestured for me to head on out to the kitchen. Once I'd taken a seat at the island and he got to work pulling out and prepping the stuff he needed for the meal, I realized that I hadn't checked my phone all night. I pulled it out of my pocket and saw that I had a missed call from my mom. I felt a weird flush of anxiety at seeing her name on the notifications.

I brought up the voicemail app and let the smartphone transcribe, but with her accent, it had some trouble. I hit play and brought the phone to my ear.

"*Hello, darling. I got your message. I didn't know you were investigating the Lamour Mansion. Um . . . there are some things we should talk about. The short answer is, yes, I may know what those words mean. Or can at least give you some information on their origins. I wish I could talk to you about all this in person, but your dad and I are actually out of town. Call me when you get this and can. Love you.*"

Well, that was strange. Pax came over to the island and tapped the counter in front of me to get my attention. "Hey, what's wrong?"

"I'm not sure. Mom left me a return voicemail in response to my message about the whole *apple* thing and the name *Seiko*. Here, listen to this. It's . . . kind of odd. But given the whole blood-type thing, I may be projecting." I put the phone on speaker and played the voicemail for him.

"No, she was definitely hesitant, and the tone of her voice when she brought up the house was peculiar, too," he said. "It almost sounded like you being there scared her for some reason. Do you think she knows something about what's going on at the estate?"

"I can't imagine why or how," I said. But after the days we'd had, nothing would shock me anymore. "I'll give her a call after we get some shut-eye." I looked at him. "This may be an out-there request, but would you mind being there with me? I have a bad feeling about what might happen during the conversation, and I'd just rather not be alone."

"Of course," he said. "Oh, crap." He hurried back over to the stove to check the omelet, and I chuffed a laugh.

"Is it salvageable?" I asked. "Sorry to distract you."

"That's a common occurrence."

Huh? I looked at his back, wondering what he'd meant by that. We were quiet for a while as he finished our breakfast and then served us both. We even ate in companiable silence. Pax and I had been working together for years, and I considered us friends, especially since Dev paired us together on investigations more often than not when they needed all-hands on deck. But I'd never really grasped how comfortable I felt with him. It was strange to realize that now.

Once I'd helped him clean up, I found myself fading. I unearthed another jaw-cracking yawn and stretched after I hung up the dishtowel.

"We should try and get some sleep," Pax said. "I'm not sure what today will have in store for us at the mansion, or what Dev will want to do given everything that's happened."

"Yeah, I'm beat."

"There are fresh sheets on the spare bed. Do you need some water?"

"That'd be good, just no holy water," I said and stretched again.

"Very funny." He brought me a bottle from the fridge and then moved to the kitchen doorway, standing with his hand near the switch. "After you," he said.

I shuffled past him and headed for the bedrooms. I could almost feel the weight of his stare on my back and gave myself a little internal shake. If I wanted to initiate something with Paxton, I knew he'd be receptive. I didn't know much about his dating history, but I knew he had seen women over the years, and he was no longer a priest. Nothing precluded him from engaging in the sins of the flesh. I grinned at that thought and was glad he couldn't see my face. I'd have to sleep on that. I hadn't dated anyone in well over a year, and Pax had been a constant in my dreams of late —the non-nightmare ones, at least. Maybe I should just throw caution to the wind and ask him out. Or jump his bones. I mean, I was a big girl and confident in myself and my sexuality. The worst he could do was reject me. And I'd get over it if he did. It wasn't like it would change anything with us working together and being friends.

Once we reached the doorway to Pax's room, I stopped and turned to face him. His glacial eyes took me in, and I felt my breath hitch a bit. While the color was like the Ilulissat Icefjord in Greenland, the heat in his stare was anything but cold.

"Goodnight, Sky," he said.

"'Night, Pax."

"If you need anything," he said, "I'm right here. Don't hesitate."

"Okay, thanks."

He reached up and tucked a stray piece of hair behind my ear and then quirked up a corner of his lip as he nudged my chin with a knuckle. "Sweet dreams."

With that, he entered his room and softly closed the door.

I wasn't sure about sweet, but my dreams would most definitely be hot—unless my nightmares followed me, that was.

CHAPTER 14

~Paxton~

I woke to the sounds of screams and flew out of bed, rushing out of my room and into Schuyler's at the end of the hall. I opened her door with a crash and found her tangled in the sheets, thrashing and struggling, battling some unseen foe and calling for help.

I immediately went to the mattress, pulling her to me and assessing the situation. The minute we connected, she calmed and relaxed. Almost too much. I worried that she had lost consciousness. "Sky? Can you hear me?" Her breathing was steady, but she remained lax and unresponsive.

"Sky. Please open those pretty eyes for me." I said a

silent prayer and brushed the sweaty strands of hair away from her face, willing her to wake. "Sky?"

Her eyelids fluttered, and she finally opened her eyes, looking up into my face. The muted light through the window cast half her face in shadow, making it hard to read her expression.

"Pax?" she said, seeming a bit confused.

"Oh, thank God. Are you okay?" I asked.

"Um . . . I think so. What happened?"

I shook my head, a frown creasing my face. "You don't remember? I woke when I heard you screaming and rushed in here. You looked like you were in the fight of your life. You don't remember any of that?"

"Now that you mention it, my throat is kind of sore, and not from my neck, and I feel even more bruised all over." She sucked in a breath. "*Sssst.* Ow." She moved away from me to sit and clicked on the bedside lamp before tugging up the hem of her T-shirt. She had three raised, red welts on her stomach and side, the lines cutting right through her tattoo. She looked at me, and I saw the discomfort in her eyes. Her logical brain might want to explain this away, but she couldn't.

"I must have scratched myself in my sleep."

I reached out and grabbed the hand still holding her shirt, pushing it so she'd lower it as I looked her square in the eyes. "Sky. I think if you dig deep, you'll realize that you didn't do this. And given what I walked in on here, we have way more to worry about than just a few scratches." I let go, and just as I did, the outlet behind Sky sparked, a small flame falling and igniting the rug.

"Shit," I said and rushed over, tearing off my shirt to tamp out the fire before it could really catch hold, mumbling another prayer as I did. Seemed whatever had been attaching itself to Sky had caused her to be stressed enough to cause some poltergeist activity.

"Pax!" Sky exclaimed. "When's the last time you had your electricity checked?"

"The electricity is fine, Sky."

"Clearly, it's not, *Pax*. I know a good electrician that I can send your way. For now, maybe we should flip the breaker for this room."

I turned to her. "I understand that your brain doesn't really work this way, but I know you've seen and experienced things you can't explain, too. And I know you've seen the movies. Given what happened to us the last two nights at the Lamour Mansion, I am begging you to open your mind. Everything we've been experiencing has been signs of demoniacal oppression. The smells, the telekinesis, the liquid, the fire. And given that it's progressed to inflicting bodily harm, we need to take this seriously. We need to go on the offensive, not the defensive. And, for some reason, this thing has a hate-on for you in particular. We need to get to the bottom of that before things escalate even more." I wouldn't tell her that *she* was causing things to happen now because of everything that had been going on. She had enough to deal with and she didn't handle this stuff all that well as it was.

She just sat there for a minute, and I worried that I'd pushed too hard. But then she nodded a bit, surprising me. "I'm not saying I believe in this, but I can't deny that *something* is going on, and that I feel personally attacked. I'm willing to entertain the idea that we need to be more careful and dig a little deeper. But the whole concept of this being a demon is still ridiculous to me."

I knew I couldn't push more. Not yet. And if she was willing to take steps to protect herself, that was all I could ask—for now. Deciding to cater to her more practical side, I used a different tack with what I wanted next. "Well, since this room clearly isn't safe, I don't really want you sleeping in here."

"I can take the couch," she said.

"I have a California king, Sky. There's no reason we can't bunk together. Besides, the doctor said you shouldn't be alone tonight."

"Can I paint your toenails and braid your hair?" she asked, and I laughed.

"Not much hair to braid, and unless you brought that black polish you're so fond of, we're out of luck there, too. How about just a promise of a good night's sleep?"

"I haven't had one of those in weeks," she said.

"I can whip us up some hot chocolate, maybe spike it with some Irish cream, and we can see if we can make it happen tonight. Deal?"

"Yeah, okay. But only if you have marshmallows."

"No marshmallows, but I'll do you one better and give you a dollop of fresh whipped cream."

"Straight to my heart, Pax. Straight to my heart."
She smiled.

The sun had already risen by the time we were
ready to head back to bed for a couple of additional
hours. Dev had texted and told us not to come to the
mansion until an hour before sunset tonight. Said they
were doing some things to protect us, and that Hanlen,
Harper, Burke, and the ghost crew were digging into
some things. Since we didn't have anything we had to
do but rest up and prepare, that's what we would do.

I woke to heat. Sweet, soft, cherry-blossom-scented
heat. Sometime during our slumber, Sky had snuggled
against me, making me the big spoon to her small. My
knee was between hers; my arm tossed over her waist.
Her hair was like a fan on the pillow, and I rolled into
its softness, smelling the sweetness of her shampoo.

I knew I should move, but I just didn't want to. I'd
gotten the best rest I had in ages in those few hours,
and even now, Sky dozed peacefully. Given what she'd
told me had been going on with her of late, I didn't
want to disturb her. She needed the sleep.

I shifted some of her hair away from my face so I
wouldn't sneeze and wake her and then put my arm
back around her, pulling her against me a little tighter.
I tensed a bit when she stirred, afraid I had woken her,
but she only sank into me more. My body came alive,

and I bit my lip to keep from groaning aloud. The woman only had to flash me a smile or throw me a sassy comeback to turn me on. *This* was something else altogether. Temptation and sin.

I closed my eyes and tried to drift back off to sleep. We could both use a few more hours if we could manage it. Unfortunately, just as I felt myself falling off that cliff into oblivion, Sky stirred once more. I figured she was likely dreaming, but the *why* of it didn't change the fact that she had begun moving against me, the sweetest sounds I had ever heard coming from her lips. I felt her breathing quicken, sensed her body heat rising, and wasn't sure what to do. Should I move away? Should I pretend I didn't notice? Should I . . . help? I mentally shook my head at the thought.

"Pax?" she sighed, her voice husky and breathy with sleep and lust. And, sweet Jesus, the sound alone had me close to the edge. If she was dreaming, *I* was in those dreams. And what self-respecting male—or female for that matter—wouldn't feel a bit of pride at that? I may be a God-fearing man, but that didn't mean I was a saint. Far from it.

"Mm, Pax," she said again. This time, I couldn't hold in my groan, and my fingers curled reflexively, fisting in the shirt she wore. She arched her back and rubbed herself more firmly against my thigh, her sweet bottom cupping the very evident proof of my desire for her. I couldn't have stopped the hiss that escaped if my life depended on it.

When she grabbed my hand and brought it under

her top to her breast, squeezing her fingers over mine as I cupped her, I saw stars. Maybe I was the one who was dreaming. Her perfect nub brushed my palm, and I felt the jolt of lustful electricity all the way through my body. When I flicked a thumb over her nipple, she arched into my palm and rotated her hips more, once again sighing in pleasure.

I should really stop this. She clearly wasn't in her right mind. Just as I was about to do just that, she slid her hand behind her back and cupped me through my boxers, squeezing just slightly, and making me see stars. That wasn't the movement of someone still asleep. That was aware, deliberate. Intentional.

"Sky?" I whispered, burying my face in her hair. If she were still sleeping and this was all a product of what I could only assume was one hell of a sex dream, she likely wouldn't reply, and I could save us both a lot of embarrassment and awkwardness by removing myself from the situation and going to take a cold shower—a *very* cold shower.

Instead of answering, she slipped her hand inside my boxers and gripped my length, running her thumb up, over, and around my crown and making my breath hitch. *God help me.*

"Sky," I tried again. "I don't think you know what you're doing. Wake up now, pretty girl."

"I know perfectly well what I'm doing, Paxton," she answered, her voice still breathy and husky but this time very, very aware. Sure. As were her hands as she continued deftly stroking me, making my eyes cross, and my entire body tighten.

God in Heaven. What should I do now?

"Touch me, Pax," she said. "Please. Just touch me. The only time I feel like myself lately is when you do. And I need to feel like myself again. I need to feel alive. I need to forget the bad shit that happened the last couple of days."

I may have been able to walk away had I not heard the near desperation in her voice. That, coupled with the way she still held me as if I were her touchstone, was my undoing. I groaned and squeezed her breast again, eliciting a gasp from her. When I moved to the other side, she arched into my touch and shifted to grip my hip, pulling me against her.

I ran my hand down her tight abdomen to the waistband of the shorts she wore, being careful of the scratches across her tattoo, and said a silent prayer as I slid beneath the elastic to the very heart of her, finding her slick and hot and oh so swollen. *God Almighty.*

"Yes," she breathed. "Please."

I slid a digit between her folds, playing with her, teasing just a bit. When I made small circles over her bundle of nerves, her hips matched my movements. When I slid my fingers inside, and she cried out, her body clenching, I almost came. I stretched her, pleasured her, felt her come alive in my hands . . . literally. But this wasn't how I wanted this. I needed to see her lose herself. I had to watch the rapture wash across her features as she shattered.

Just as I sensed she was close, I withdrew.

"Goddamn it, Pax," she said, her voice full of frustration, and I chuckled a bit. I couldn't help it.

"He has nothing to do with this, my sweet." I flipped her to her back, fitting myself between her thighs as I quickly brought both of her hands above her head with one of mine, effectively caging her beneath me. The position brought us even closer, and I saw her pupils dilate as she gasped.

"I need the words, Sky. I need to know that you want this. That you *really* and truly want this. Want me." I ran my other hand down the side of her face, melting a little inside as she leaned into the touch, before swiping my thumb across her full bottom lip.

"It's all I want right now," was all she said as she stared me directly in the eyes, and that was all I needed. I let her go and reverently stripped her of her clothes, paying attention to all the places revealed as I did, and then I got rid of what little I wore, too. When we were both in only what God had given us, I finally leaned in for my first taste of her lips.

Her taste was sublime, and the feel of her under my hands was a blessing I never thought to receive. She had been temptation for a while, and this was a sin I was more than happy to commit.

Our tongues dueled, our breaths mingled, and I never wanted the moment to end. When I made my way down her body and sampled her honeyed heat, I realized she tasted like the apples on her tattoo—sweet and tart and tempting. Utterly alluring. Completely sinful.

She came apart for the first time, and I gazed upon her face. If ever an angel existed on Earth, Schuyler Liu was it. She was gorgeous, breathtaking. Heavenly.

And right now, in this moment, she was all mine.

CHAPTER 15

~Schuyler~

When I could breathe again—barely—I took stock of where I was and what was happening. Paxton Chase had just given me the most intense orgasm of my life, and we'd barely just begun—at least, I *hoped* we had only just begun.

His body was a work of art, a runner's physique with a bit of gym-body definition. His skin was like silk under my hands, and I didn't want to stop touching him—though I had to admit, I wouldn't complain if he wanted to restrain me a bit again because . . . damn, that was hot.

He leaned over and pulled something from his nightstand drawer. When I saw the silver square, I plucked it from his fingertips. "Uh, uh, uh. Not so fast," I said. He raised an eyebrow at me as I pushed him to his back and straddled his waist, running my gaze down his body.

When my lips followed the trail my eyes had taken, he shivered and groaned. When I took him into my mouth, he gently fisted my hair in his hand—not to force my movements but to connect us in yet another way—and it was the hottest thing I'd ever experienced. I worked him, sliding my tongue up and down his length and cupping him, making him pant with need.

"Sky, you need to stop, or this is going to be over before it even begins," he said.

"Duly noted," I said and ripped open the foil packet, sliding the condom down his length. Even that was sexy as fuck, and I couldn't wait to see what happened next. Just as I was set to settle myself atop him and take myself on what I assumed would be the ride of my life —with a *priest*!—he surprised me by deftly flipping us and resuming control. My breath caught, and I could only stare, the shine of lust in his eyes making my belly clench and my girl parts melt.

"Okay," I said. "Your show. Got it." He proceeded to run his hands all over me again, bringing me to the brink before backing off and then stoking the fires once more. Just as I thought I might explode, he flipped me onto my stomach, raised my hips, and slid home. I could do nothing but grip the sheets and bite the pillow. The stretch, the burn, the *pleasure* was too much. In two thrusts, he had me coming again, crying out his name.

Falling to the side and switching to something slightly more sweet and less demanding, he had me cresting for a third time. I didn't think I could take any more, but when he moved me to my back once again and retook his position, peering into my eyes as he pleasure me—pleasured *us*—I couldn't hold back the building fire. It rose to an inferno and burned out of control, just as he toppled over the edge.

Both of us slick with sweat and breathing as if we'd run a marathon, we lay there for a few minutes, trying to come back to Earth—at least, I was. Pax hadn't moved at all.

"Uh, Pax? Are you still alive? Do I need to call a friend? I don't think I have JC's number," I asked, a smile gracing my lips.

He finally picked his head up and looked down at me again. "Honestly? I'm not sure. I'm kinda thinking I may have just died and gone to Heaven."

I laughed. "Not sure your god or the saints would be too thrilled to meet you at the pearly gates in nothing but your birthday suit, but I bet any women on the other side would welcome you with open arms. Though I might have to have Dev do a spell so I could go and throat-punch someone. Just sayin'."

He chuckled as I intended and then rolled off me. The loss of him tugged at something in my chest—something I didn't want to dwell on too much right now. When he leaned over and gave me the sweetest, hottest, most complete kiss I'd ever received before getting up and heading to the restroom, I worried that I would have to face it sooner rather than later. But for now, I would bask in the afterglow. Because, oh boy, was I ever. I probably shone like a lighthouse beacon at this point. I'd just been loved more thoroughly than ever before in my life, and by an ex-priest, no less. There was irony there. Likely some really good sass. Perhaps even a joke or two. But I was too sated for my brain to come up with anything useful.

Just as I finished throwing my clothes back on, my phone rang. I checked the readout and noticed that it was well after noon and that it was my mother.

"Hi, Mom," I said, lying back on the bed.

"Hey, baby," Mom answered, and I heard the smile in her voice. "How are things?"

"Eventful." I wasn't sure I wanted to get into what had been happening at Lamour. Besides, from her voicemail, it sounded like *she* was the one who had something to say. I felt weirdly vulnerable and hoped that Pax would come back out soon. I needed an emotional support buffer, and I could think of nobody better.

"Did you get my voicemail?" Mom asked.

"I did." I drew out the word. "You sounded . . . odd. What's up?"

She blew out a breath, and my stomach clenched. I glanced at the bathroom door and tried to will Pax to return. I had a bad feeling about where this was headed, and I had no idea what it even had to do with.

"Oh, honey," she started, a tone in her voice I didn't exactly like. That pit in my stomach turned to lead. "Your father and I hoped . . . I don't actually know what we hoped. This isn't something we wanted to do. Not yet. Maybe not ever. But given current circumstances, we have no choice. I'm just sorry that we can't be there in person to tell you."

"Are you getting a divorce? Is someone sick?" I asked, and heard my mom laugh on the other end of the line.

"No, honey. We're fine. Everything's fine. There's just something we probably should have told you years ago. Something it seems has become more urgent given your job."

"You're scaring me here, Ma. What the hell?" As I was saying that, Pax came out of the bathroom, drying his hair with a towel, his sweats hanging low on his waist. He raised a brow at me, and I frantically gestured for him to join me. When he tossed the towel on the back of a chair and did just that, I put the phone on speaker, set it between us on the bed, and took his hand, looking into his eyes and shaking my head.

"Um . . ." my mom started.

"You know we love you, right, Sky?" my dad said.

"Of course, I freaking know you love me, Dad. What the hell is this about?"

I heard my mom take a deep breath on the other end of the line. "When your father and I were young,

147

we wanted nothing more than to have children. Alas, we weren't granted that gift."

"But then you had me," I said.

"Then we got you," my dad replied, and I noticed his word choice. Before I could ask about it, my mom continued.

"One late night, thirty-four years ago, your father and I were taking a walk in the Garden District. It was a beautiful night. *Piáoliang.* The moon was full, and the October air was brisk but not cold. As we approached a park, we noticed a figure running towards us, a bundle in their arms. At first, we were a little scared, afraid we'd unknowingly stumbled upon a crime." I noticed her accent thickening a bit as it did when she was riding high on some emotion. That in and of itself concerned me.

Mom stopped, and my dad took over. "It was a man. Maybe in his sixties or early seventies but hard to tell. He was disheveled, bruised and bloody, smelled of smoke. And in his arms, a wiggling bundle of cloth. He thrust it at your mother and in the most urgent and sincere voice imaginable said that we had to keep you safe. That we must not tell anyone where you came from or what had happened—even though we had no idea what *had* happened. He didn't even give us his name. Just said, 'Bless you. This is a child of light. The darkness may not have her.' And then he put his hand on your forehead, whispered something, and continued running, looking back only a few times before disappearing around the corner. I'll never forget it."

I looked at Pax and saw that his eyes were wide, likely matching my expression. He grasped my hand more firmly and pulled me into him. I soaked in his warmth. His strength. I was too shocked to even form words. I didn't even know what to ask first. Where to start. But before I could even take a breath to try, my mom jumped back in.

"You were so very perfect. Ten fingers. Ten toes. Big, brown eyes that looked upon the world with such wonder. I knew the moment I laid eyes on you that you would do great things. I never put too much stock in love at first sight until I saw you. We did some digging. Tried to figure out where you came from. Your dad used his connections, but nothing ever really came of it. DNA testing was only in its infancy and not something we could have used to try and track down your family. And all the while, we loved you and raised you as ours. We told our friends that you were a relative from China we were helping to escape a bad situation, and that we had decided to adopt you. And we did. Adopt you, that is."

I finally found my voice. "Hold up. So not only am I not your biological child, but some weirdo thrust me on you in the middle of the night outta nowhere? And you, as a lawyer, never thought to question the possible legal ramifications?"

"Well, I wouldn't exactly say that or put it that way," my dad said. "You were a gift. A precious gift. One we were only too happy to accept—and break some rules for."

"I think I need a minute."

"We understand you're confused, baby," my mom said. "And I wish I could give you more. I wish I could tell you more about where you came from and what happened. But all we were ever able to discern was that the night this all happened was the same night the massacre occurred at the Lamour Mansion. We have no way of knowing if they were connected, though. Not for sure. Or if any of what we heard and read is true. But given all the rumors about the black magic witches who lived there . . . if there was even a possibility they were connected somehow, we only wanted to protect you and keep you safe—as the man asked us to do."

"To this day . . ." My dad picked up the story. "We don't know why he had you." His voice quavered. "We don't know why he was so insistent that we take you, keep you safe, and tell no one. Or why we never saw or heard from him again. All we knew then—and now—is that we loved you and that you were ours the minute you landed in your mother's arms."

"I—" I started, not sure what to say. What to feel. "Okay, I really need to unpack this a bit. That was—*is*—a lot."

"I know, honey. And I'm so sorry," my dad said, sorrow in his tone. "We love you so much. When your mother told me that you were working the Lamour Mansion, I took it as a sign that it was time to tell you.

We know you're strong enough to handle it. But I hope you know that we never kept it from you to hurt you. We just—both then and now—had no idea what we were supposed to keep you safe from, and when my contacts didn't uncover anything, and we had fallen so utterly in love with you, accepting that you were ours, it didn't seem as important anymore."

"I know you love me, Dad," I said with a sigh. "But I need time to process. Some things happened at work, and I discovered the other day that our blood types don't match so I had a feeling that something like this was coming."

"Oh, Sky, are you okay? Why did you have blood drawn?" my mom asked.

"I'm fine. Honest. Just precautionary. But while that means this wasn't as big of a surprise as it might have been at any other time, it's still a lot. Not to mention, there is some weird-ass shit going down at Lamour. Now that I know the truth of this, it's layers upon layers of already fucked-up stuff. I just need a beat, okay? I love you both. We'll talk soon."

Without giving them a chance to say more, I disconnected and melted into Pax's hold. "What the actual fuck, Pax?"

He kissed my head and bundled me close. "I don't know. But we're going to figure it out. I'll call Hanlen in a little bit and do some digging of my own in the parish. For now, let's just settle awhile. If you want to talk, I'm here. If you just want to rest, I'm still here." He shifted and tipped my chin up with a finger, looking deeply into my eyes before taking my lips in a soft, sweet kiss full of strength and acceptance. It was exactly what I needed. And as we lay down, his bigger body wrapped around mine, I couldn't help but think that this may have been the most unexpected day in the history of the universe.

CHAPTER 16

~Paxton~

Sky had drifted off to sleep again, albeit fitfully. I figured she was likely feeling a bit hurt and stressed, and it was probably taking its toll on her already taxed body. Not to mention everything she'd gone through during the investigation the last couple of days. She'd handled the news that her parents had unloaded on her well, but as she'd said, it was still a lot, on top of a lot. And I had a sick feeling that it would only get worse.

I put in a call to Hanlen and asked her to check on a few things for me as a favor, beseeching her to keep it to herself until we got some answers—if we got any. She agreed but asked if she could at least tell Dev. I conceded, knowing I couldn't ask her to keep anything from the one she loved.

Checking on Sky once more and feeling confident that she'd be okay now that her emotions had calmed and she was inside all my protections, I left her a note and walked to the one place I knew I could find some clarity—and maybe some answers. Old St. Patrick's was a landmark in the area. A throwback to the arts of another time. A nineteenth-century Gothic wonder with a tower soaring over one hundred and eighty-five feet into the air, and massive, breathtaking murals behind the altar done in 1841. The church was one of the only buildings in the area that retained most of its original glory.

I entered the doors into the vestibule, greeted by the scents of incense and candles, the vaulted ceilings echoing each breath and making it feel as if it filled your entire being and not just your lungs. Dipping my fingers into the fountain of holy water in the narthex, I made the sign of the cross, genuflected, and slid into one of the beautifully restored cypress benches, bowing my head. While I had my issues with those who headed the Church—capital C—I had no issues with the establishments themselves. Quite the opposite, in fact. And while I was of the mind that people should be allowed to worship anywhere they chose, be it in a cathedral or the middle of the woods—and that there was nothing wrong with any of those places—something about a timeless structure full of faith and history; love, laughter, and tears, got me every time.

As I sat and prayed, I felt a presence slide onto the bench beside me.

"What troubles you, my son?"

I looked up into the rheumy green eyes of Father Duncan McLeod, one of my grandfather's oldest and dearest friends.

"Nothing, Father." I looked down. "Okay, that's not entirely true. Quite a bit is weighing on me right now." I looked at him again as he placed a hand on my shoulder, the warmth in his eyes easing some of the tension in my chest.

"Care to talk about it, then?" he asked, his Irish accent thick even after all these years of being in the States.

"Most of it is probably better left for confession." I smiled. "But I do have a couple of questions for you if you have time to answer them."

"Of course, son." He looked around the nave. "I haven't seen any parishioners besides you in hours. I have some good Irish whiskey in my office. Care to join me for a wee nip?"

"Now you're talking, Father. And maybe not so small. After the couple of days I've had, I could use a generous pour. It's five o'clock somewhere, right?" He smiled, and I followed him beyond the altar area to the sacristy and then to his office at the rear of the building.

It was small but nicely appointed with a cherry wood wardrobe cabinet and desk as well as a set of leather armchairs. He gestured for me to take one and then went to pour our drinks, coming back to hand me one and take the seat across from me.

"What's on your mind, Paxton?"

"Grandda," I said.

He made the sign of the cross and nodded. "Oh, aye. Rest his soul. It's glad I'd be to talk about my dearest mate. I do miss him so."

I took a deep breath and moved forward, reaching into my back pocket to pull out my phone. When I unlocked it, I went to my photos and brought up the one I needed, handing the cell to Father McLeod.

He set his whiskey glass on the side table next to him, donned his reading glasses, and took the device, taking a moment to study the picture, zooming in to read the text. I waited for him to finish and gauged his reaction. He didn't seem surprised.

Duncan knew.

"You knew," I said. "You knew that he was the priest involved with the Moon Call Coven massacre. Did you know where he was when he disappeared from my life, too?" I asked, feeling a bit of my Irish temper rise.

Duncan pursed his lips and nodded, taking a deep breath and letting his shoulders fall on the exhale. When he met my gaze, I saw the sorrow in his expression. I also saw the regret. "Aye, son. I did. Dougal was a good man. A very good man. He didn't do what some thought he did. He had nothing to do with any of those deaths. He *saved* lives that day. He ultimately sacrificed himself to safeguard those he could."

I shook my head. "I don't understand. Why did I

never know this? Did Da know? *Does* he know?" I asked.

He tipped his head back and forth, side to side, and then reached for his glass to take a sip of his whiskey. "I believe he knows some. Not all. Nobody knows all. Not even me. But I know enough, I do. I know enough to know that Father Dougal McGuire singlehandedly stopped an evil coven of Satan-worshipping witches from sacrificing more innocent lives and ultimately ended up paying for it with his life. God rest his soul." He crossed himself again.

"Wait, do you know more about how he died? I don't believe for one second that he took his life. He never would have risked his soul like that."

"I do not believe he did, either. No. But I also do not know all that happened on that Montana mountain pass. I only know what had been happening to and with him after the events at Lamour."

"I think you'd better tell me all that you *do* know, Father. Fill in some of these blanks for me. Because we are investigating the Lamour Mansion for *Haunted New Orleans* and have encountered more than we ever bargained for already. I'm afraid to see what might happen next, and the research on the history of the place has been much too slow for my liking. The facts we've uncovered have been incomplete, and the theories inconclusive. I need to plug some of these holes and make sure that my team and I are safe. Since I can no longer talk to Grandda about it, and Da seems to want nothing to do with me because of my falling out with the archdiocese, you're my only hope."

"Okay, my boy. I best be refilling our glasses, then. This is a tale one does not share or receive clear-headed."

* * *

HOURS LATER, I was finally on my way back to the house, my head spinning and mind reeling. I couldn't believe everything that Father McLeod had shared. About two blocks away from home, my phone rang. I pulled the cell out of my pocket to see Hanlen's name on the screen.

"Hey, Hanlen," I said.

"Hey, yourself," she replied. "So, I got some information for you."

"Yeah? I just got a boatload of information myself."

"You did?" she asked.

"Yep. I went to see my grandfather's best friend, Father Duncan McLeod at St. Patrick's. All those holes that we couldn't fill in regarding the Moon Call Coven massacre and the priest? Well, I just filled in a ton of them."

"Wait a minute. I'm confused. That's not what you had me looking into."

"No, it wasn't. But . . . I think it's all tied together."

"O-o-o-okay. Hold on a second. I'm going to put you on speaker so Dev can hear." I heard a clatter on the other end.

"Hey, Padre," Dev said.

"Hey, boss. Okay. So, the other day when Harper came by the estate to drop off her research on the history of the place, I saw something in her printouts that really shocked me. I didn't say anything at the time because I didn't know what to make of it, and we ended up talking about something else and then I didn't have a chance. Anyway, the deep dive she did into the priest from the Moon Call Coven massacre? That sheet with the picture of the priest involved that everyone was always so careful about not naming or sharing? It was a photo of my grandfather. Dougal McGuire."

"But your last name's Chase," Hanlen said.

"Yeah. I legally changed it in my twenties. After everything that happened with the exorcism and the excommunication, I figured it was for the best. I went to my mother's maiden name so I could effectively distance myself from the Order and my father. You know we don't have the best relationship, even though I know we can call on him if we need him. He may be a crappy dad, but he's an excellent priest. It's really too bad we can't just use Duncan."

"Wow, Pax. I'm so sorry," Hanlen said.

"It's honestly okay. My mom was the rock in that relationship. When we lost her, I knew it was inevitable that things between my dad and me would fall apart. But that's not what this is about."

"What exactly *is* this about? Because the things I

dug up today kind of blew my mind. I'm not sure I can handle much more," Hanlen confessed.

"As the write-up said, Grandda was the priest present at the massacre thirty-plus years ago. But unlike the theories, Duncan—Father McLeod—told me that Grandda actually saved lives that day. He didn't kill anybody. Seems the Moon Call Coven was in the habit of sacrificing children. Newborns and infants predominantly. When Duncan told me the story, something from my demonologist training came back to me. Back in the day, black magic covens used to boil baby fat and then mix it with herbs and crushed crystals to rub onto the skin. They believed it gave them power and allowed them to commune more easily with their dark patrons."

"Jesus," Hanlen said, just as Dev gasped.

"*Merde.*"

"You can say that again. Anyway, one of the young coven members who'd left the *family*—and I use that term loosely—contacted the Church about what was going on at the estate. She didn't feel comfortable going to the police because she had been involved, but when she broke free of them, she felt she needed to do something. She told Grandda that they had a big sacrifice planned for the night of the blood moon, and he took it upon himself to go and break it up. It was stupid—"

"And reckless," Hanlen interrupted.

"Yes, and reckless, but that was Grandda. If he thought there was even a snowball's chance in hell of doing some good, he'd do it. Consequences be damned."

"I see where you get it from," Dev said, and I smiled.

"Anyway, from what Duncan told me, when Grandda got there, the ritual had already started. They had an infant on an altar, a big copper tub behind it, and their black priest was ready to murder the poor thing. Duncan told me that Grandda said that when he walked in, psychokinesis was in full effect. Things were levitating, there was an unnatural breeze in the room, the sound of a marching band could be heard coming from everywhere and nowhere, and the smell was something straight out of a defunct butcher shop. He said the place had all the earmarks of a demon infestation. I won't go into detail on the stories that Duncan told me Grandda told him, but suffice it to say it was something I hope we never encounter—though I fear we already may have sampled some of it."

"Why do you say that?" Dev asked.

I took a deep breath and leaned against the nearest building, letting my head fall back and bending a knee to prop one of my Chucks on the brick behind me. "Because I am now convinced that our inhuman spirit, the one we keep encountering at the mansion, the one that attacked me and Sky and Aaron, is the same one the coven worshipped back in their day—and maybe even before since we know the property was handed down through a family."

"So, what happened after Father McGuire got there?" Hanlen asked.

"Duncan told me that he went in spiritual guns blazing," I laughed. "Grandda was a demonologist, as well, and a well-recognized one. He traveled all over the country and did a lot of work with Ed and Lorraine Warren—I'm sure you've heard of them."

"Uh, yeah. Who hasn't heard of the most famous paranormal researchers in quite possibly the world?" Dev said.

"Wait. Aren't they the ones from that movie about the doll?" Hanlen asked.

Dev laughed. "Yes, babe. And countless other horror books and movies. They were very, very real. Hollywood just dramatized their experiences for the big screen."

"Wow," Hanlen said, and she actually sounded impressed. "Padre's family ran in famous circles." She laughed. "What happened then?"

I continued. "Duncan said that Grandda was able to beat back some of the evil, enough to make it to the altar. When he disrupted their circle and rite, it caused all sorts of havoc. Apparently, the dark things they'd conjured and called didn't take too kindly to not getting what they had been promised in the time they were promised it and started attacking the coven members. Duncan told me that Grandda said it was a bloodbath. If they weren't being attacked by things he couldn't see, then they started attacking each other. Killing one another. He barely got away unscathed. But he didn't leave before he did one very important thing."

"He saved the child," Hanlen breathed.

"He saved the child," I echoed.

"I think you should pick up Sky and come over to the plantation. Right now," Hanlen said. "We have a whole lot to discuss."

"That's what I figured," I said. "She's actually still at my place. At least, I hope she is. I convinced her to spend the night because of her injury and what happened at Lamour. She was sleeping when I went to the church. I'll pick her up, and we'll see you in a few. You might as well call the rest of the team in, too. It'd probably be best to only tell these stories once and then form a game plan for the rest of this investigation. Because I don't think we've seen the worst of it, and that's saying a lot."

"I one hundred percent agree, Padre. Get Sky and come on out. We'll take care of gathering everybody we can."

"Okay," I said. "See you soon."

CHAPTER 17

~Schuyler~

I was just finishing my makeup and hair when Pax walked into the bedroom.

"Hey," I said, turning and gesturing to him with my mascara wand, "did you get what you needed from god?"

He chuckled. "When I said I was going to the church to see a friend, I didn't mean God, but yeah, I did."

"Oh? Who did you go and see?" I turned back to the mirror and put the final stroke on my left lashes and then put the tube back in my bag.

"Father McLeod. He was my grandfather's best friend and was kind of like a godfather to me growing up."

"Oh, that's nice. Even if he *is* a priest," I said and carried my stuff out to put it back in my larger bag. When I turned to look at him again, I saw the tension in the set of his shoulders and the lines on his face. "What's wrong?" I asked. "I didn't mean anything by the priest comment."

"No, it's not that. We've uncovered some things about the house. I just talked to Dev and Hanlen on my way home. We're all meeting at the plantation to go over everything. Are you almost ready?"

"Yep. Just need shoes." I took my boots out of my bag and slipped them on, taking time to properly criss-cross the ribbon laces and loop them before tying. I glanced back up at Pax where he stood leaning against the doorjamb and saw that same look. "This is more than just info on the house," I said. "Do you regret last night—or this morning, rather?"

"What?" he said and hurried over to me, cupping my cheek in his palm. "No. Oh, no. Not at all. Never. Do *you*?"

"Nope," I said with a smile and turned to kiss his palm before continuing with my other boot.

He took a step back so he wasn't crowding me, and I sensed that he had more to say. I peeked up at him again. "But?" I asked.

"No buts. Not really," he answered. "But here's the thing, Sky. What *are* we?"

I shook my head and looked back down. "Do we need a label? Can't it just be two people enjoying each other? Friends with benefits—even though that *is* a label?"

"Enjoying," he said, and I sensed that maybe I'd said the wrong thing. But then he continued. "That's present tense with a promise of a future. Does that mean that what happened wasn't a one-time thing for you?"

I stood and walked closer to him, looping my arms around his neck. "I'm game for more if you are," I said and leaned in to kiss him. Sweetly. Passionately. "But I'm also not big on titles or labels."

He nipped my lower lip and then pulled back a little. "Sadly, I kind of am."

"That's because you're old-fashioned," I quipped and lowered my hand to squeeze his very bitable ass before moving to my bag on the bed. But then I couldn't help but tease him a little more. I glanced over my shoulder at him. "Or is that just old?"

It had the impact I hoped for. He lunged, taking me to the mattress and eliciting a squeal out of me as he tickled me, nipping and nibbling on my neck and my ear.

He sighed. "I'll show you just how *not* old I am later. But for now, we really do need to get to Arborwood." He lifted himself off me and then helped me to stand.

"That's a shame," I said with a wink, but then brushed by him to leave the room.

Pax was quiet on the drive to the plantation house, and I wondered what was going through his head. He kept casting furtive glances at me and didn't seem to want to let go of me, constantly running his thumb over the back of my hand as he drove. This was more than just what'd happened and was continuing to happen with us. I just didn't know what it was about.

When we pulled up to the house, I saw nearly everybody's car. "Wow, when you said the team, you meant it. This must be big," I said.

"Lots of stuff has come to light." And that was all he said. Nothing more. My stomach did a little flip, and I wondered what was up.

When we walked into the courtyard, I saw that everybody was in the outdoor seating area we'd set up for the premiere of the Arborwood episode wrap party. It was beautiful outside today, and I was glad that we were enjoying it. "Hey, guys."

Everybody looked up from what they were doing or stopped talking and turned to us, issuing waves and hellos.

"Looks like the gang's all here," Hanlen said.

"You can say that again." I gestured around at everybody. "Pax said that we got some information on the house. Must be big news."

"Very big," Dev said and kissed Hanlen on the temple as he moved to the other side of the big table to grab some cheese from the charcuterie board someone had set out. "Grab something to eat and drink if you're hungry or thirsty and let's settle in. This may take us a minute and we need to discuss what's going to happen at Lamour tonight, too."

Pax and I did as Dev asked. Once everyone was

sufficiently settled, Hanlen got up and stood in front of us.

"Okay, so . . ." she began. "I got some information, Padre got some intel, and Harper uncovered some things. What we've discovered since is that they're all related." She looked at Pax and Harper; both of them nodded, and then she looked at me. I wasn't sure why she was looking at me, but when Pax moved closer and slung his arm around the back of the couch and across my shoulders, that funny feeling in my gut turned sour.

"Okay, guys. What the hell is this all about? You're all acting like the other shoe is about to drop and fall right on *my* head, and I've kinda had enough lately." I crossed my arms and raised a brow.

"Sky . . ." Hanlen started. "Padre told us about what you found out regarding your parents." She looked around at everyone. "Dev filled everybody in on that bit before you guys arrived. We're so sorry."

"Oh, is that all? It's fine. Really. They're still my parents, and I actually understand why they didn't tell me. I'm not having an identity crisis or anything. Sure, I need to unpack it a bit and decide whether I want to know more, but it's really all good."

Hanlen nodded and shared a glance with Dev and then peeked at Pax. "Well, *do* you want to know more?"

"You make it sound like you can tell me more."

She smoothed her ponytail and propped her hip on the arm of the oversized outdoor chair, taking a half seat. Then, she just looked me in the eyes and nodded. "I'm not sure who should start with this story," she began again. "Padre, do you think it'd be better for you to tell your bit, for me to tell mine—which I haven't even told *you* yet—or for Harper to share her news?"

Pax rubbed my shoulder and I felt myself relax, though marginally. "I might as well go. I can bring everyone up to your piece, at least."

He then proceeded to tell everybody about Father Duncan McLeod and his grandfather and how he'd just found out that his granddad was the priest at the center of the Moon Call Coven massacre. We all just stared in shock. I looked around the courtyard and saw everybody—all those who didn't already know—with the same looks on their faces. Once he'd finished, he looked back at Hanlen and then at Harper, seeming to ask the silent question of who wanted to go next.

So . . . Pax's *grandfather* was the one there that night? Now I knew why he'd looked so familiar in that picture on Pax's wall. I'd seen him in Harper's paperwork.

"I think maybe I should go next," Harper said, and we all turned to her. "So, I was doing some more digging into the estate's history, specifically related to the dark coven. Burke gave Dev some leads for me to follow up on, and it led me to something huge." She stopped and looked around at all of us.

"I found and talked to a member of the Moon Call Coven—well, an *ex*-member—who didn't die on that fateful October night. Back then, her name was Shelly Masterson. Now, she goes by Michelle Higgins. She was one of the youngest members of the coven but was able to get away from them before they got their hooks in too deep." She reached into her messenger bag and pulled out a folder, flipping it open on her lap and leafing through the sheets of paper.

"That fits with what Duncan told me, too," Pax said.

"She actually left the compound in March of that year and went into hiding, recording everything she could remember about her time with them at Lamour and what they had been doing and planned to do. Seems their leader, a"—she peeked down at the papers again—"Lance Palilonis, was into a whole lot of sacrificial murder. And he preferred it to be personal." She looked up at all of us again.

"As we know, there were upwards of eighteen people living there at one point. Most times, it was thirteen, the perfect number for a coven. But here's the kicker. Lance liked his witches a little too much. He had relationships going with a bunch of them and sired several children."

"But we didn't find any record of children," Dakota said, and Harper looked at her, the look on her face indicative of what I knew was about to come next.

"Exactly," she said. "And do you want to know why? Because Lance thought that sacrificing infants and children—*his* children—would earn him favor with the dark one they worshipped. None of them lived past the age of two."

"Motherfucking asshole," Aaron said and slammed a fist into his opposite palm. "If the fucker weren't already dead, I'd want to take him out."

"You and me both, brother," James said and held out a fist for a bump.

"Well, that explains the sorrow and pain I felt in that house," Birdie said, and all the other sensitives in the group nodded. "And you guys may get your chance,"—she looked at Aaron and James—"because I am going to send the asshole to the abyss for good. I *know* he was one of the presences we felt at Lamour."

Harper nodded. "Michelle told me that the coven had a rite and ritual planned for the night of the blood moon, which was"—she checked her paperwork again —"October 7th. They were supposed to sacrifice the newest infant. Another of Lance's offspring. A baby girl."

Everybody gasped, even me. But then it hit me. "Wait," I said. "Didn't the massacre happen on October 8th?"

"It did," Harper confirmed. "The police arrived sometime after four a.m. on the morning of the eighth to find everybody in the house dead, and the back of the mansion smoldering." She looked at Hanlen. "Do you want to pick it up here?"

"Yeah, sure," Hanlen said and stood again, starting to pace. "I was looking into something related but slightly different. Sky asked me to help Harper look into the *apple* reference and the name *Seiko* that came up, and Padre asked me to dig deeper into your past, Sky."

My breath caught. I looked at her and then at Paxton, finding his gaze intent on mine. "I'm sorry," he said. "I should have asked for your permission, but I had just found out about everything with my grandfather, and I had a hunch."

I wanted to be upset at him for not talking to *me* about it first, but I knew this hadn't come from a place of malice. He was only trying to piece things together, likely for my benefit. "It's okay," I said and saw the relief pass over his face. I turned back to Hanlen. "So?" I asked.

"So . . ." she started, smoothing her ponytail again before pacing some more. "When I accessed the databases I use for Arbor Investigations, I came up with something that I think both explains everything and opens up a whole new can of worms." She looked at me.

"Seiko Chen was a member of the Moon Call Coven. She became a member at a very young age when her mother emigrated from China and joined during Lance's father's rule. As Harper told us, Lance liked to sire offspring on his members to be later used as sacrifices. Seiko was one of those witches. She had a daughter. A girl she told people close to her outside of the coven she named . . ."—she looked at me—"Apple."

My breath caught. My tattoo. *That* was an interesting coincidence.

"So, the EVPs we got during the investigation were legit?" I asked, and everyone nodded.

Harper chimed in. "Elliott told me the other day at home that she had been playing in the receiving room with a woman named Seiko the morning I brought her here, and that Seiko's boyfriend, Lance, had asked her to stay at the mansion."

I shivered. *Predator, much?* Even in death. This was all way too fucking weird. "So, we know the Seiko and Apple references now, and we know that the coven's high priest—or whatever he was—was named Lance. And that Pax's grandfather was the priest who was there the night of the massacre. That's all great, but . . ."

Hanlen took a deep breath and came to sit on the coffee table in front of me, reaching out to take my hand. My first instinct was to rip it away. I felt really vulnerable all of a sudden and wasn't exactly sure why. And it made me angry. But I held steady and let Hanlen say whatever it was she had to say.

"Sky," she began, looking directly into my eyes, "we were able to piece together everything. Padre's grandfather did save lives that night. Michelle's, since she likely would have been killed by someone in the coven for defecting and then blowing the whistle on them, and the child's—the baby they'd been set to sacrifice. The little infant girl. Apple. Whom Dougal took away from Lamour and entrusted to someone. Someone he found in the spur of the moment but believed would do right by her. And I think if you let that big, beautiful brain work it out, you'll get to where we're going with this."

I felt the world fall out from under me, and everything close in at the periphery. I barely registered Hanlen holding my hand anymore, Pax's arm snug around my shoulders, and everybody staring intently at me where I rested on the couch.

"Are you saying I was meant to be fucking baby fat body lotion?" I couldn't hold back the snark. Because . . . seriously?

"Well, that got dark fast." She quirked her lip. "But, yes, we confirmed it. I had a friend run the DNA. They had most of the coven members' DNA on file from after the . . . incident, even though they couldn't test it at the time. The samples were still intact. Seiko Chen was your mother, Sky. Padre's grandfather saved you that night and gave you to the Lius."

Dev walked up behind Hanlen and put a hand on her shoulder, looking at me. I rose my gaze to meet his ocean-water stare.

"And now, Lance, your . . . well, let's just call him your sperm donor since I don't think he deserves anything nicer, wants you dead, and this dark presence want you back."

"Where's the child?" I whispered, remembering what we'd heard on the Geoport.

Well, fuck.

CHAPTER 18

~Paxton~

A few hours later and three-quarters of a shared bottle of whiskey at Hanlen's suggestion—for those who weren't teetotalers, anyway—we sat around the large dining room table at Arborwood, working out the details for our night-three investigation. While we had a show to finish and obligations to the network to see to fruition, we also had souls to help, and an evil to vanquish—one that wanted to reel Sky back into its clutches and sink its claws into the rest of us along the way.

"Okay," Dev said, "Birdie and I did some work at the estate this morning. It should offer us some additional protection, but now that we know that one of ours is essentially a trigger object, we'll have to step up our game." A trigger object was something that the spirits used to influence our world. Generally, it was something from their life before. In this case, Sky was Seiko and Lance's daughter—two of the spirits we knew haunted Lamour, and one of whom we knew was malevolent. She had also been promised to the demon the Moon Call Coven worshipped, which meant the demoniacal intelligence likely felt entitled to Sky and her soul.

I rubbed a hand over my nape, palming the scapular I still wore, wishing for the thousandth time that I'd been able to get it directly from my grandfather before he died. That I'd had more time with him. More time to learn from him, too. He could have taught me so much about exorcism and all the minutia of being a demonologist that I had yet to experience. I wasn't sure that I was up for however this might play out alone, but I really didn't want to call in my father. I figured it might be good to get Dev's and Lark's opinion.

"Dev? Birdie? Do you think the three of us—with everybody else's help, of course,"—I looked around at the entire team—"are up for this? I . . . I don't really want to call in my father unless it's absolutely necessary. Not to mention, I don't think we actually *could* with the Church requiring all the proof before they even sign off on any kind of official exorcism."

Lark walked over to me and gently laid a hand on my shoulder. "We understand, Padre. And I think we can handle it. Plus, tonight's just about finishing up the investigation and doing what we can. If things don't go as planned, we can call him in later—and we may have to do exactly that, because I have a feeling we are going to need to get rid of this thing once and for all. But, personal things aside, inviting the negativity of the animosity between you and your father into the home, especially now, probably isn't the smartest thing. And your dad's a closer tie to the priest who thwarted the dark entity, too. That may just piss it off more."

"I agree," Dev said and nodded. "I've got my magic and spells, Lark has hers, and you will bring your blessings and prayers. We'll make sure everyone else watches out for Sky."

"I can take care of myself, thank you very much," Sky said from my side, her tone brooking no argument. I looked at her and felt something in my chest clench. I didn't want her anywhere near the mansion tonight, but I knew we couldn't keep her away. Still, I would have a talk with her later. In private.

"Hey, doc?" Dev said.

Harper looked up from her paperwork. "Yeah, boss?"

"I was thinking," he said. "How would you feel about putting all the non-magical team members under hypnosis—with their permission, of course—so that Birdie and I can work a small spell and give them some extra protections and some temporary sensitivities?"

"I can absolutely do that," she said. "But, like you said, it has to be everyone's choice."

"Of course," Dev answered. "I'd never ask any of you to do something you're not entirely comfortable with." He looked at Sky then, and I turned to gauge her reaction. Of everyone, I figured she might be the most hesitant. But she surprised me.

"I'm down," she said and shrugged. "It's science, right?"

Dev smiled. "Science *and* magic, but, yeah, it'll begin with science."

"Honestly, I'm halfway to crazy town already. Everything that has happened to me during this investigation—and even before—along with everything I just found out about my life? I'm tired. I'm tired of fighting. Tired of trying to make sense of it all and fit it into neat little boxes of the things I believe—or *don't*. I'm just gonna go with the flow here for a bit and then sort out what's left after." She looked at me.

"Are you sure?" I whispered, worrying a little at how all over the place her emotions seemed. First, she sounded accepting, then defeated, then almost angry. It wasn't like her, and I wondered if she was feeling beaten down more by the entity's influence than she was letting on.

She nodded. "Yeah. Let's just get this over with." She got up and walked away then, and Dev moved to follow.

"No," I said. "Let her go." I looked over to see Larken smiling widely, the look on her face reminiscent of the cat who ate the canary. "What?" I asked.

"Oh . . . nothing," Lark answered and smiled wider. "Your aura is just nice and pink."

Dakota peered at me, too, and I started feeling a

little self-conscious. "You're right. And I think it's more than just his faith." The two women shared a look and some sort of silent communication.

"Okay, ladies. Stop reading my colors. Is nothing sacred?" I felt both relieved and a little resentful that a bit of what I felt for Sky was out of the bag.

"Oh, plenty's sacred," Dev said. "Especially this." He winked and walked away, taking Hanlen's hand as he did and gesturing for Myst to follow them, leaving me groaning inside. I had no problem with the team knowing that Sky and I were romantically involved— or at least intimately involved. I wasn't so sure how *she* would feel about that, though. I took a deep breath.

"What did I miss?" Van asked his sister, and Lennie just shrugged.

"Your guess is as good as mine," Aaron chimed in, and James and Turner just shook their heads. Harper only grinned and kept going through her paperwork.

"It's not important," I told the group and then ran a hand through my hair. "I need to go and prepare. I'll be in the garden out back if anybody needs me."

Everybody nodded or voiced their acknowledgment, so I moved to the double doors at the back of the house and then through them out onto the porch. The garden with its fountain and benches sat directly in front of me, and I moved to it, taking a seat to be amidst nature. I pulled out my rosary and started with my prayers and meditation, preparing myself for the night to come.

Just as I was finishing, Van, Halen, and Turner came

outside. "Hey, Padre," Van said. "We're headed out. Harper worked her David Copperfield mojo on us, and then Dev and Birdie did their woo-woo. We're gonna head to Lamour to make sure everything's set with the equipment for tonight. By the way, the doc told me that if you were done, you should go in. Dev and the rest of them want to view the footage of the attic from the other night if there's time, too."

I had forgotten all about the cameras up there. I wondered if they'd caught anything when Sky was dragged up there and assaulted. Just the thought of it had my blood running cold again.

"Got it," I said. "Drive safe, guys. And be careful. I know it's still light out, but I don't like the idea of anybody being there alone right now."

"We were given strict instructions never to be alone," Lennie said. "And based on what's happened so far with no explanation, I'm totally cool with that. I don't plan to be the final girl anytime soon. I'm too pretty, much too scrappy, and I've got way too much to live for."

Van and Turner laughed. "Yeah, no Jamie Lee Curtis-ing for you," Turner said, and they all waved and headed through the gate in the side of the yard. I took a couple of deep breaths and then went inside.

I caught a glimpse of Harper in the sitting room with Dakota, Hanlen, Aaron, and James. The doctor's soothing voice, and the tick of the metronome almost made me yawn. I heard Dev and Birdie talking some-where on the ground floor, but with the echo, I couldn't tell where they were, exactly. I looked around some more. I didn't see Sky anywhere.

Taking care not to be too loud and disrupt Harper's hypnosis session, I made my way outside and through the inner courtyard to the front yard, thinking I might know where Sky had gone. When I made it outside, I rounded the building and moved past the carriage house to the rear of the property near Bea's cottage and then to the cemetery beyond.

As expected, I spotted Sky nearly right away, sitting on a bench in the middle of the little plot and looking out over the small pond that someone had created who knew how long ago. Lily pads floated, and the trees around and draping over the surface created interesting, dancing shapes on the water like moving artwork, interrupted by the ripples caused by the slight breeze.

Sky had let her hair down, and it blew gently, floating in the air and caressing her back. I sat down beside her without a word and simply pulled her against me, one arm wrapped around her shoulders. She melted into my side and rested her head on my pectoral. I felt her draw in a deep breath and then slowly let it out.

"How are you holding up?" I asked.

"I honestly don't know, Pax. On the one hand, I really am okay with the fact that I'm adopted . . . And I'm grateful that your grandfather saved me from being melted down and used for the fuck knows what. *He* saved me, not god." She smiled a bit, and I returned the expression.

"But finding out who my biological parents were, what kind of *people* they were . . . *On top* of everything that's already happened, it's kind of messing me up. None of it is information I can easily sort or explain, and I haven't even had a moment to process, let alone come to terms. You know?"

She pulled back a bit to look at me, and I tucked her hair behind an ear. "It seems that everything lately has been falling into the unexplainable category. Not to mention, I haven't felt like myself in nearly any capacity in weeks. I'm usually pretty comfortable in my skin. I'm unashamed and unapologetic about who I am and how I am. But some of the things I've been thinking lately, how I've been feeling . . . they don't really,"—she paused for a beat—"fit," she finished, and my stomach did a little flip.

"Are you talking about us?" I had to ask.

A look of surprise crossed her face. "Oh, no. No, Pax," she said and moved closer, grabbing my hand with hers. "If anything, that's the only thing I *have* been good with lately. Being with you makes me feel normal. It makes me feel more vibrant and alive than I have in weeks. Your touch is the only thing that soothes me lately and makes me feel halfway okay."

I thought on that a minute. I knew what she meant. Even gentle, innocent touches had calmed me lately, as well. And I'd noticed how she relaxed when I made contact, especially during the high-stress moments at Lamour. I had to wonder if there was more to that than just our connection. Did my faith somehow negate the evil trying to gain a foothold in her? Maybe Dev or Birdie would know.

Sky squeezed my hand, bringing me back to the present moment, and we both looked out at the pond for a minute. I leaned over and kissed her on the top of the head. "We should probably get back in the house. Harper was finishing up with Dakota, Hanlen, Aaron, and James, and once Dev and Birdie do their thing with them, I know they'll want to finish up with us. Are you up for it? Actually, are you up for this period? Not to be overprotective, but I really don't want you anywhere near this tonight."

She smiled softly. "I'm not running from this, Pax. It's personal now. Literally. I need to see this through, whatever that looks like. Does it make me uncomfortable because I can't keep it all neat and tidy? Hell, yes, it does. I mean, fuck. What *is* half of this, even?" She chuckled. "But life is sometimes messy. And when I get a moment after this to go over everything that's happened, I will file it away in the places it needs to be and then get started on the next phases. As for the hypnosis, I mean . . . as long as she doesn't make me cluck like a chicken, and they don't *magic* me into believing in god or anything, yeah, I'm good." She flashed me a grin and a wink, and I leaned in.

We kissed, sweetly yet hotly, and then I pulled her in for a seated hug. I felt my chest squeeze. Sky was becoming someone incredibly special to me, and I hoped that she could feel that.

I marveled at how quickly things had changed for

us. We had been friends for a while, but there was always a pall of uncertainty over our relationship. Dev partnered us during investigations more often than not —he liked to put the faithful with the nonbelievers wherever possible and had told us way back when that our energies meshed well, too—but I never really knew how Sky felt about me, and I was always too afraid to really let myself show her how I felt, especially with our age difference. With this investigation, all of that had flown out the window. It was like we'd finally let each other *find* one another, and that had led to us feeling what we probably should have been feeling all along.

I wouldn't push or rush her, though. Sky was head-strong, and if I put too much pressure on her, I was afraid she'd balk—or worse, run. While I liked and wanted labels, she was worth the discomfort I might feel at not having them.

I released her and stood, extending a hand. "Shall we?"

She placed her hand in mine, and I helped her to her feet. "We shall." She chuckled.

We made our way back to the plantation house and inside to the sitting room. Dev and Birdie were just finishing up with Dakota, Hanlen, Aaron, and James. The spell they worked seemed to be an easy one, just combined energies, some burned herbs, and a few strategically placed crystals. I didn't really consider myself a sensitive at all, at least not like Dakota and Lark and Dev were, but even I could feel the static charge in the air and the buoyancy. It was an uplifting feeling and made me feel strangely safe and protected as well as energized. I found that I was kind of excited to see how different things would feel and be after they literally worked their magic on us.

When they finished, Dev glanced over at us where we'd stopped near the doorway. "Hey, guys. Just one second and we'll wrap things up with you two." He looked at the group still seated on the couch. "How do you feel?" he asked.

Hanlen stretched. "I feel great. Relaxed yet energized. Focused." She looked at the others. "You?"

Dakota and the cameramen agreed. "So . . . these *sensitivities* you said you were giving us. What does that all entail?" Aaron asked.

Dev sat on the arm of an oversized chair. "It's kind of like the spell I did for Hanlen after we investigated here but a little more powerful. What I did for her was allow her to hear the ghosts. Her head injury is what allowed her to see them. What Lark and I just did for all of you was to temporarily allow you all to see *and* hear them like we do, as we do. With that said, the rules still apply. You will only see them if they want to be seen. You will only hear them if they say things that can be heard within human range. Any of you who are slightly more sensitive naturally may get more psychic flashes and may hear more in your head like Dakota and Lark do already. It'll be pretty personal. Each person will likely be different. But, the bottom line is, we wanted you to be prepared. If there's a chance for you to see or hear something before it happens tonight, we wanted you to have that protection."

"I'm all for that, especially after what happened with Padre and Sky." James looked at us. "How long will it last?"

Dev looked at Birdie. "Probably about thirty-six hours," she said. "Long enough for us to get through the investigation and wrap up anything we need to do after."

Dakota got up and cracked her back. "I'm ready to rock and roll. I have to do some things to prepare for tonight, so I'm headed out." She looked at Aaron and James. "Do you guys need a ride back to the city?" She turned to Hanlen. "Who's taking the other van to Lamour tonight?"

"We'll drive over in my SUV later," Hanlen said. "Aaron and James should take the other van. So, if you want to head out now and go home quick, the time is yours." She smiled.

"All right. I'm off. I'll see you guys in a couple of hours." Dakota waved as she left, and then Aaron and James said their goodbyes, as well. Knowing them, they'd probably hit up a barbecue place and binge before tonight.

Harper gave us a long look. "Are you two ready?"

"Ready as I'll ever be," Sky said and took a seat on the couch.

I sat next to her and quickly squeezed her knee before letting go. "Let's do this."

CHAPTER 19

~Schuyler~

I tried to relax. I really did. But the minute Harper started the metronome and began talking, something in me . . . revolted. That was the only way I could explain it. I felt anxious. Uneasy. Those strange voices in my head started up again, and an odd sense of anger rose without any rhyme or reason. I had chosen to do this. Nobody was doing anything to me against my will. Why, then, did it feel like my subconscious was screaming at me to stop?

I started when I felt a hand on my elbow. I opened my eyes and looked up to see Harper crouched near me, her hand still in place. "Are you okay, Sky?"

"Sure. Yeah. Why?" I asked.

"Because you haven't stopped fidgeting since I

started. Your foot's been bouncing, you've been clenching your fists on your thighs, and while your breathing should be deep and even by now, it's still choppy. Not to mention, your face is full of tension." She traced a fingertip across my forehead and then dropped her arm.

Pax reached over to grab my hand. The minute he touched me, I felt myself relax a little.

"Interesting," Dev murmured, and I glanced at him across the room.

"What?" I asked.

"Literally the second Padre touched you, your aura shifted, and you visibly calmed."

"I saw it, too," Birdie said.

I looked at Pax, and he stared earnestly at me, his baby blues full of compassion and . . . something else. Something I didn't have time to think about right now.

He threaded his fingers through mine and gave my hand a little squeeze. "Are you okay with me holding your hand while we do this?" he asked and then looked at Harper before shifting his gaze to Dev and Birdie. "Is that okay?" he inquired.

"I think we might have to," Dev said, and Larken nodded.

Harper returned to her spot by the metronome in front of us, and Pax squeezed my hand again and then settled back against the cushions. I did the same, wiggling myself down until I was comfortable. There was still a bit of an internal . . . pushing going on, for lack of a better way to describe it, but I did feel more at ease, and the strange whispers had quieted.

"Okay," Harper said, her voice melodious and soothing. "I want you both to close your eyes again and focus on the sound of my voice and the ticking of the metronome in the background. Feel your bodies sinking into the cushions. Feel each toe relaxing, one after the other. Feel your ankles loosen. Feel the muscles of your calves get heavy. Notice how your thighs unclench and become weightless."

She took a breath. "Breathe deeply with me as your glutes and hips and lower back release any and all tension you may be holding there. Feel your middle and upper back first clench and then relax as your body feels warmer. Heavier. The muscles in your shoulders and biceps and arms and hands become so heavy, you can barely feel them where they lay. Notice how the muscles in your neck lengthen and loosen, making your head heavy. Let it droop as all tension leaves your face. Unclench your jaw and feel the lines in your forehead smooth, your lips parting."

I breathed deeply as she instructed and felt warm and heavy and content. I still felt a bit of a rustling in my chest, as if anxiety wanted to rise from somewhere but couldn't, but it was negligible now and easily ignored.

"Your body is warm and heavy. You're sinking into the couch, feeling relaxed and calm and safe. Let your mind drift," Harper instructed. "Let your thoughts go to a place where you are open to suggestion, knowing that you are cared for and looked after. Safe. That the things you are instructed to do will not hurt you. How do you feel?" she asked.

Pax and I answered. I honestly wasn't sure what either of us said, but I know we replied.

"Okay, when I count to five, you will be receptive to the magic that Dev and Larken do. You will feel comfortable and accepting. You have free will to withdraw and wake up if anything *doesn't* feel right to you. Do you understand?"

"I understand," I murmured.

I sat there, breathing deeply, feeling light, weightless, and open—almost oblivious to everything but how great I felt now after weeks of feeling like garbage.

"One. Two. Three. Four. Five," Harper counted, and I felt myself relaxing even more. Floating. I wondered if I was even still awake. Was I dreaming?

"Okay, open your eyes," Harper instructed.

I did as she said and felt utterly relaxed and yet hyper-focused. Almost like those moments right after a really great massage—or good sex. It was amazing.

"Wow, girl," I said. "You should totally do that more often and charge the big bucks for it. That was better than a day at the spa."

Harper smiled, and Pax squeezed my hand. "You feel good?" he asked.

"I feel freaking fantastic," I said and grinned.

"Yeah, I feel pretty great, too."

I looked up at Dev and Birdie. "Are you guys going to do your thing now?" I asked.

Dev smiled, and Lark laughed a bit. "We already did," Dev said, and Birdie nodded.

"Wait." I felt my brow furrow. "You already did your . . ."—I flapped my free hand—"whatever the hell you were doing?"

"Yep," Birdie said and walked over to a sideboard to pour some water from a pitcher. "We're all finished. You guys are good to go." She returned to us with two glasses of water, and Pax and I each moved to accept one. Pax let go of me—and the world dropped out from under me. Just like the glass in my hand.

Intense, cataclysmic pain ripped through my head and chest, making both seize and stealing my breath. I curled in on myself and grabbed at my skull. The voice was back, louder than ever, and yelling hateful things now. Telling me to do things that I would never even think, let alone contemplate, even on my worst days.

I heard a scream. I didn't know if I had screamed or if it was someone in my head. All I knew was pain. Rage. *Hate.* I heard a growl and worried that it came from me, but I didn't know which way was up right now, let alone what the hell was happening. I heard more glass shattering somewhere. Heard banging and crashing and thumping. My eyelids felt glued together, and I registered the discomfort of having my eyes squeezed shut so tightly. I was totally unable to pry them open, even to see what was going on.

I thrashed. Threw punches. Snapped and snarled. I knew that much, but I didn't know why and I couldn't stop myself. I felt as if someone else were controlling my body. My mind. My voice.

I didn't know how long any of it took or how much time had passed. It felt like both an eternity and a heartbeat. Suddenly, I registered a subtle pressure on my shoulder and then . . .

Nothing.

*　*　*

I WOKE with my head pillowed by a lap and looked up to see four people standing around me, looks of extreme concern on their faces.

"What—?" I started, my voice cracking, and my throat dry and sore. I tried again. "What the hell just happened?" I asked.

Pax smoothed my hair and ran a hand gently over my face, gazing down at me, his eyes so startlingly bright in color now, he looked almost feverish. Speaking of feverish, I was hot. Much too hot. I felt almost . . . sunburned in a weird way. Or windburned. As if all the moisture had been stripped out of my body.

"Water," I croaked and tried to sit up. Pax held me in place but motioned to the side, and I saw movement out of the corner of my eye and heard someone leave the room. A minute later, Hanlen returned and handed me a bottle of water, the top already twisted off.

Pax helped me to sit up a bit but didn't let me move too much and didn't allow me to move away. At this point, I was just fine right where I was. I had no idea what the fuck just happened, and I honestly thought I might be losing my damn mind.

I took a few gulps of the water, the cold liquid soothing my scratchy throat and cooling me a bit. I looked around at everyone, suddenly noticing the destruction of the room. Cabinet doors were open. A wall mirror was in pieces, its frame still hanging lopsidedly on the wall. The pitcher and glasses on the sideboard looked more like glass confetti now. The big armchair that Dev had been propped against earlier was turned halfway around. Other furniture seemed shifted, some teetering unnaturally as if legs or supports or something had been broken.

"Anyone feel like filling me in?" I asked.

"We're not sure *exactly* what happened," Pax said and ran his hand down my arm. "We think the hypnosis may have opened up something in you. A window or little door that the dark entity exploited."

"Whoa, whoa, whoa. Slow your roll. There is no 'dark entity' in me."

Dev moved closer. "Sadly, we think there might be. Its influence, anyway. We've talked about the oppression before. This thing has sunk its claws in you. It's affecting you outside of the estate. Those dreams? The physical malaise and health issues you've been experiencing? The mood swings . . ."

"That's likely why you felt twitchy and looked so tired after our first visit to the estate. That's probably when it happened. And even the stuff that happened at my place after the hospital, Sky," Pax added.

"What about that night?" I asked.

"All the things that happened to you in the bedroom? The horrible night terror, the scratches, the fire in the outlet?"

"Yeah," I said. "Nightmares and bad electrical. What about it?"

Pax shook his head. "It wasn't that. But because I knew you were okay, I didn't push. It *was* poltergeist activity, Sky."

I laughed. Like outright, belly-laughed despite the situation. "So, what?" I asked. "You have a Casper?"

"I don't have anything," Pax said, and the look on his face was super-serious. "My house is fortified. I'm not sure anything could get in, even if it tried."

"Then what the hell are you talking about?"

Birdie sat on the coffee table near the couch so she was closer to eye level with me. "Do you remember when we discussed the different kinds of hauntings way back when you first joined the team?"

"Yeah. Well, some of it anyway. A lot of it just went in one ear and out the other." I glanced at Dev. "No offense, boss."

He smiled. "None taken."

"Well, what do you remember about what we said about poltergeist activity?"

I racked my brain, trying to remember what had been said. "Floating objects, mischievous goings-on . . ." I said.

"And?" Birdie prompted.

I thought some more. "Um, I remember you guys talking about how the jury was still out on what exactly causes the activity."

"Exactly," Dev said.

I looked from him to Birdie. "I'm still not getting it."

"So, the disconnect," Lark started, "is that some parapsychologists believe that spirits are responsible for the physical and psychological disturbances. However, another subset of people believe that poltergeist activity is actually—"

"Unknown energy caused by a living person under duress or stress." I finished and then couldn't stop myself. "So, basically attention whores playing pranks."

"It's not at all," Pax said, and I looked up into his eyes.

Dev sat next to Birdie on the table, and Harper and Hanlen moved in closer. "If we go with the second option there, that poltergeists are actually psychic energy created by people to cause telekinesis and telepathy on an unconscious level, then I'd say being tormented in your sleep for weeks would be enough to cause that to happen. Not to mention your history. You come from a long line of black coven witches—on both sides—Sky, whether you want to admit that or not. You're . . . *extra* in your DNA. I know this is all woo-woo nonsense to you, but it is what it is. You were quite literally born into this world, and this thing, whatever it actually is, has had it out for you since you were an infant."

He stopped for a minute and looked away, a strange expression filling his face. "I'm sorry about all this happening to you. I feel absolutely terrible for not protecting you better. I shouldn't have sent you guys in for that initial look-see without at least some kind of protection—just in case."

I jerked forward, my head swimming just a little, and reached out to take Dev's hand. "Stop it. Don't be stupid. This is my *job*, Dev. This is what I chose to do with my life. You didn't *make* me do anything, and it's certainly not your fault. You only try to help people. Be it by proving to them that they need to call a contractor and get some shit fixed or giving them something to believe in so they can calm their fears. This isn't like any other case we've done. There are *way* more unexplained things going on here than usual. But, again, not your fault. So, stow the guilt. It's misplaced."

"Thanks for saying that," he said and flashed me a smile, though it didn't quite reach his eyes.

I took a breath, feeling Pax's hands tighten on me where he still touched me. "Okay, so . . . beliefs aside, I want to at least try to understand what *you* all think. You're saying that this dark entity—god, I feel stupid even saying that out loud, and *why* do people who don't even believe in gods still use that turn of phrase? Anyway . . . —you're saying that this thing has affected me enough in some way that I am now going all X-Men when I don't even realize it?"

"Simple but effective thought process and description there, Sky. I like it," Hanlen said, and Dev just shook his head.

"In the simplest terms . . . yes. And I think that opening you so much with the hypnosis and the spell backfired a bit and made you even more susceptible temporarily. When you were out, Lark and I did some energy work on you, and we think we calmed things down, but we honestly won't know for sure until we test it out."

"And how do we do that?" I asked, a bit of a scoff in my voice, even though I liked the idea of experimentation.

"I need to let you go," Pax said, and I felt a weird shift in my belly. It had nothing to do with what was going on and everything to do with the completely unrelated meaning to those words. I shoved it into the back of my head with all the other things I'd need to work through later and turned to him a bit more.

"Okay, let's test it." I moved away a little and stood, still holding Pax's hand. Dev, Harper, and Hanlen took up places around me, assumably to protect me in case anything happened. I looked down at Pax and met his eyes as I slowly slipped my hand from his.

I felt a bit of pressure in my head and chest, but things were quiet, and I seemed okay.

"So?" Dev asked.

"It's like it was before. Like it's been. I get a weird pressure, and it causes me to feel a little tired—kind of like having eye strain but in your whole body—but I can function fine."

"Okay, good," Birdie said and nodded her head, a look of relief sliding across her face.

"I really don't want you there tonight," Pax said, and I looked at him again where he still sat on the couch.

"Well, it's a good thing that it's not your decision, then."

"Schuyler . . ."

"*Paxton*," I mocked, and the corners of his lips quirked as he shook his head.

I flopped down on the couch next to him and took his hand, looking him square in the face. "I appreciate your concern, I really do." I looked around at the others. "All of you. But this is my fight now. More than I ever wanted it to be. I don't know what will happen. I don't think I'll understand most of it. It's probably going to keep my mind occupied for ages after this investigation, trying to figure out the whats and whys and hows, but I'm in this now. This involves my history, something I didn't even know I had until recently, but I need more details, more facts, more evidence. I need to gather as much intel as I can to research later. This is what I do. It's who I am. I need to be there. Can you understand that?"

He nodded slowly and looked down, quickly brushing his thumb across the back of my hand. "I can understand it,"—he looked back up into my eyes—"but I don't have to like it."

"That's fair," I said and let go of his hand, standing again to test out how I was feeling. I would be okay. I felt pretty much like I had earlier in the day—sadly.

That hypnosis high had been freaking nice. It sucked that it had gotten ripped away so fast.

I checked my watch. We didn't have much time before we needed to convene at Lamour. "I need to go and clean up before tonight, and I'm sure none of you will let me head home alone," I rolled my eyes and then looked at Pax again. "Can I use your shower?"

"Of course," he said and stood.

"When you guys get to the estate," Dev said, "we'll take a peek at the footage from the attic when you were dragged up there, Sky."

"Gre-e-e-a-a-t," I said, and everybody laughed.

Paxton and I said our goodbyes and headed out of Arborwood to Pax's truck. He was quiet on the way to his place, but he didn't let go of my hand.

Not even once.

CHAPTER 20

~Paxton~

We pulled up to Lamour just as the sun was starting to turn the sky a wash of colors. It was gorgeous. God's artwork more beautiful than any artist could capture on canvas. We grabbed our gear and headed inside, neither of us saying much.

When we entered the mansion, I felt a thickness in the air. It could have been a bit of anxiety. The fact that I knew we'd likely have an interesting night ahead of us could have played a role. But the very space itself seemed anticipatory. Like a murderer watching from across the street as his next victim walked in front of a bedroom window while on the phone, completely unaware of what lurked outside.

I glanced at Sky. She seemed to tense a bit as we

entered the foyer, but she otherwise seemed okay. I'd have to keep an eye on her.

We made our way to the parlor where all the equipment was still set up. The team looked up from whatever they had been doing and gestured and said hellos. After we stowed our gear, we made our way over to the monitors where Turner sat with Dev.

"Hey, you two," Dev said. "We were just getting the reels queued."

Turner fast-forwarded through a bunch of footage from the attic, periodically looking down at a notebook that he had next to him. Suddenly, he glanced back up and stopped the forward motion, pausing the video on an empty shot of the attic room and just the very top of the stairs.

"Okay, this is it, I think," he said and turned to Dev.

"You stopped it right at when we marked the time from the Handycam and the EVP recordings?"

"Actually, it's several minutes earlier. Thought it might be good to see if anything happened *before* Sky got tugged up there. Especially since the monitor went black the night of the investigation and we didn't see anything," Turner said and then stood. "Someone else can have my chair. I'm gonna go and grab some water. I'll be back in to take a peek, but you should be fine without me to do whatever you need to do next." He walked out of the room.

I turned to Sky. "Do you want to sit? There might not be too much opportunity for that tonight, and this might be hard to see."

"Yeah, okay," she said and took the chair that Turner had vacated.

Hanlen, Dakota, Aaron, and James all gathered around, and I scanned the space. "Where's Birdie?" I asked.

Dev looked up and out the archway. "I'm not sure. She must be taking care of something. I can fill her in later if needed. Van and Lennie are looking at some of the equipment in the back of the house and I don't want to bother them right now. It's not super important for them to see anyway. They already reviewed all the data from the JumpBox, the Geoport, and the Wonder Box to make sure that everything was working well electronically when we received what we did." He turned to us. "You guys ready? We have it set up in slow motion so we can catch things better, so this may look a little weird—and probably even scarier. But I want to be able to mark things to enhance after the investigation, and we can always watch again in normal speed later."

He clicked the mouse, and we saw and heard nothing for a minute, just some dust motes floating across the field of the night-vision camera. Suddenly, however, I caught movement in the corner and looked over to see . . .

"Holy shit," Sky gasped, and those behind us exclaimed, as well.

I couldn't have said it better myself. There, in the corner of the attic, was a figure. A full apparition, nearly as *real* as we were in the moment. It was a female, dressed in a black cloak with the hood down. Given the way things appeared in night vision, her hair and eyes were probably dark. She had a petite build and looked . . . anxious.

Dev quickly paused the video and looked at all of us, turning to take in those behind him, too. "You guys see that?"

"Holy fuck," Aaron said.

"I'll take that as a yes." Dev chuckled. "I guess our hypnosis and spell worked," Dev said and then turned back to the monitors, pressing play once again.

The figure remained, wringing her hands and looking around frantically. Suddenly, another apparition popped into existence next to her. A tall, slender male wearing the same kind of cloak as the first figure. He seemed to have light hair and eyes. He turned to the first form and said something, his features pinched in anger and frustration. While we couldn't hear what was said, we could intuit the gist. He was very unhappy with the female.

He gestured wildly around the space, pointing his finger at the woman and then at the stairs. When the female moved towards the stairwell, he grabbed her by the arms in what looked to be a bruising, crushing grip and shook her, his eyes narrowed in rage.

We all gasped, and Dev paused the video again. "If I had to venture a guess," he said, "I'd say that's Seiko and Lance." He turned so he could see Dakota. "Have you gotten any psychic insight?"

"Nothing specific. More just . . . feelings. And I have to agree with you."

"So, those are my biological parents," Sky breathed, and I reached out and squeezed her shoulder. She let me; even raised her hand across her chest to place it over mine, but she never took her eyes off the frozen image on the monitor. "Either that, or I have a brain tumor. Might be more plausible."

Dev looked over at her. "It's not a tumor." Aaron and James laughed, and it took me a second to realize that it was a movie line. Dev just shook his head and then asked Sky, "Are you okay?"

"Yeah, I'm fine," she said.

"But you know what happens next," he said. "This isn't going to get any easier. And now that you know that you can see the spirits, I don't know what that will mean for what we might witness next."

She turned to him. "I'm fine," she snapped, and I squeezed her shoulder a bit. "Let's see what we might have to deal with tonight."

"Okay." Dev pushed play again, and the figure we believed was Lance pulled the woman we thought might be Seiko into a chokehold, holding her against his body so she couldn't get away, but making her face the stairs. Just as he did and whispered something in her ear, we saw phantom footsteps appear in the dirt and dust of the floor, leading to the stairs. We couldn't see a body attached, but there were definitely footprints there—long, huge feet with claw marks. It reminded me of the water we'd found in the hall, and I tried to remember what the shape of those looked like.

Then, we heard the screams on camera.

I tensed, and most everybody said something. The shrieks sounded even more blood-curdling in the slower speed, and I felt my stomach bottom out a bit. We watched, in slow motion on screen, as Sky's hair appeared first at the top of the stairs and then the rest of her body, bit by bit. She thrashed and fought, screamed and swore, before sliding across the floor and slamming headfirst into the wall with force and speed—even in slow-mo.

Sweet Jesus, that could have broken her neck.

"*Merde,*" Dev said and paused the video again to a chorus of:

"The fuck?"

"Oh, Sky . . ."

"What did I just see?"

Dev scrubbed a hand through his curls and shook his head. "Well, I think it's safe to say that inhuman entities follow the same psychic rules. They're only visible if they want to be. It's probably even more accurate with an entity of that kind of malevolence and intelligence." He looked around at all of us. "But that means we'll have to be extra careful tonight."

He turned to Sky and looked her straight in the eyes. I felt her tense beneath my hand. "We know what happens next. Are you sure you want to see this?" he asked.

Sky took in a deep breath and then let it out slowly.

"I mean, it's not like I want to see myself get strangled, but I *need* to see. I need to see what *else* I might see. Does that make sense?"

"It makes sense to me," I said and squeezed her again. And it did. Given Sky's personality, she likely needed to see this, especially now that she knew she could witness more than the average person—even if she didn't quite understand how, and likely hadn't processed it yet.

Dev nodded solemnly and pushed play again. We watched as Sky tried to get up, only to be slammed back down. We watched as she clawed at her throat, scissoring her legs and scraping her heels against the wood floor. We watched as Lance made Seiko watch, and Seiko dissolved into tears, shaking uncontrollably in Lance's punishing hold.

We heard Sky tell whatever had her that it couldn't hurt her, and then we heard the most bone-chilling thing of all. A voice that sounded as if it had been scraped from the bowels of Hell, screaming, *"no."* Then, in a guttural voice that trailed off, "I *will* have you," before Sky suddenly flopped down. Sky had never mentioned hearing that when this all happened. I wondered if it *couldn't* be heard by the naked ear.

Just before we heard the footsteps on the stairs as I rushed up to her, we heard something else.

"Our daughter belongs to him."

"Fucking hell." I didn't know who said it, but it was absolutely accurate.

Fucking Hell, indeed.

Dev looked at Schuyler. "I'm so proud of you for remembering what we taught you and taking charge in such a terrifying moment, Sky. You showed incredible bravery there." He smiled. "We're going to get to the bottom of this, and we'll kick this thing's ass. I promise you that."

She only nodded her head.

CHAPTER 21

~Schuyler~

*W*e all took a minute to absorb what we had just seen and then went about our normal tasks of preparing for the last night of investigation. I couldn't help wondering what tonight would be like—and how it would change me. Forever. I mean, I had been hired to be one of the show's skeptics. To use science to disprove things. To be the yin to Dev and Birdie's yang, so to speak. Would I even have a job after this given everything that had already happened?

Even now, seeing the figures on the screen when I *knew* they hadn't been there at the time it'd happened was a complete mind fuck. Not to mention, I had—wrongfully, it appeared—assumed that the spell only worked on things in person. I had a feeling this was only the beginning of the things that I might see or experience tonight that would shake my foundation to its core.

I took a bit longer than usual gathering my things and readying myself for the team meeting we always had right before we started for the night, thinking over everything I had just seen and what Dev had said. I still felt the pressure inside me and that overwhelming sense of being watched and not being alone—and it had nothing to do with my friends in the room with me.

I peeked over at Pax where he knelt near his bag, going through his stuff. I saw his lips moving and figured he was probably saying some prayers for tonight. It wasn't often, but occasionally—*very* occasionally—I wished I had some faith. A belief in something other than what I could see and touch and measure. I figured there was some comfort to be found there in giving up control. I likely wouldn't even think that if it weren't for Dev and Larken and Paxton and their very steadfast faiths and beliefs.

I checked my watch and saw that it was just about time. Dev walked into the room, and we all came to attention.

"Okay, guys. Birdie and I talked it over, and we don't want anybody going anywhere alone tonight. In fact, we'd like to keep the groups to four." He looked around the room. "Padre? Sky? Are you guys good heading to the back of the house tonight—the kitchen, dining room, butler's pantry, and that back area with the exposed storage space? You can take Aaron and Birdie with you." We both nodded and sought out Aaron where he stood on the other side of the room. Lark still wasn't in attendance, and I hoped that everything was okay.

"Hanlen, you're with me, and we'll take James and Dakota upstairs." Hanlen gave Dev a thumbs-up, and James nodded.

"Van, Lennie, Turner, Harper, I want you here in Control. And, as I said, nobody goes anywhere alone. Harper, Len? You gotta pee, take a buddy. Same goes for the guys."

Van raised an eyebrow at the newest member of our team. "I'm not sure I know you well enough for that yet, bro," Van said, and Turner shook his head and turned a little pink.

"Believe me, man. That's the last thing I wanna see."

Everybody chuckled.

"Oh, hey, guys," Dev said with a smile, and I frowned. He'd just been talking to all of us, and I didn't know what he—

Holy shit.

Five figures appeared in the archway to the parlor, and I had to sit down. So, I did. I just slunk right down to the floor where I had been standing and stared, my heart pounding and my palms sweating.

Deep breaths, Sky. You're fine. You're okay.

Dev smiled wider and gestured to the newcomers. "Team, I'd like for you all to officially meet my sister, Wren,"—he indicated to a gorgeous woman with long,

silky twists, wearing a white, off-the-shoulder dress—
"her guy, Findley,"—he pointed to a handsome man
with perfectly styled hair and dark Irish good looks—
"my cousin, Gunnie,"—a beautiful woman wearing a
bustier and a mini-skirt waved, her black-and-purple
braids shifting—"and Desmond." A young man in full-
on vintage soldier attire gave us a little bow.

"You all know Burke." Our historian smiled and
moved closer to Gunnie—or Reagan as Hanlen knew
her—putting his arm around her shoulders. He still had
his surfer-boy good looks, made even hotter by the
glasses he always wore. Even in death, apparently. I
mentally shook my head. I still couldn't believe that
we'd lost him to a serial killer. And I *really* couldn't
believe that I was seeing him again now—and that I
wouldn't be able to see him again after this investigation.

Any of them.

"The gang is *really* all here," Hanlen said, and everybody laughed—even the ghosts.

Ghosts. Did I honestly just think that? But what else
could I call them? I knew I wasn't dreaming. I knew
that this was the anticipated result of the hypnosis and
the spells that Dev and Birdie did, but I couldn't
completely wrap my head around it.

Holy shit.

I opened my eyes wide, took a deep breath, and
glanced over at Paxton. He awkwardly raised an arm in
greeting to the ghost crew, a look of absolute shock on

his face as he palmed the back of his neck with his other hand.

"Do you have any information for us?" Dev asked, his question directed toward the newest arrivals. Would I hear them if they talked? Dev said we might be able to. I knew that Dakota and Lark could hear them in their heads, and Dev could always hear them as well as he could hear us. I guessed we'd find out.

"It's been a little quieter," Desmond said, and I peeked at Paxton, watching him sink to the floor just as I had earlier. I was sure this was a bit hard for him, too. He put faith in it way more than I did—pun intended—but it still went against some of the things he had been raised to believe. "I only counted four presences here last night. The others we saw early on in the investigation have been scarce."

"I wanted to do some more digging for you, Sky, but it's been hard to get Seiko alone," Wren said and then looked at me. Her eyes were gorgeous—like faded dollar bills.

"That asshole, Lance, is always with her," Findley added and pulled Wren to him, kissing the top of her head. Something shifted in me at seeing them together, still so very much in love. I looked at Pax again and felt my chest warm. It was much too soon for words like that, but I did care about him.

"And Moloch is here. Always here," Gunnie said quietly. From what I'd gathered from both Hanlen and Dev, Reagan was always a bit quiet. Even in life, despite her outward appearance suggesting anything but.

They'd said she was always a bit of an enigma that way, and I respected the hell out of that. Then what she'd said registered.

"Mol—?" I started.

"Don't!" Pax barked as he caught my gaze with his. "Don't voice its name in the land of the living. It gives it strength. You only do that if you're ready to provoke it and send it back to Hell."

Most everyone nodded or shook their heads, though the rest of the team members who weren't used to this kind of thing looked about as shell-shocked as Pax did and I felt. When my gaze found Dev, I saw the look of shock and forced acceptance on his face, and my stomach bottomed out.

He nodded solemnly. "So, you were able to uncover a name," he said.

"*I* did," Burke said, and Gunnie moved closer to him as if seeking comfort. "Moloch is traditionally a Canaanite god of child sacrifice. He appears most often as a towering figure with the head of a bull and flaming hands, said to bestow incredible blessings on the devout in exchange for those sacrifices. The problem is . . . I don't know if this is actually that deity, or if this is a demon or king of Hell masquerading as a pagan god. Since *Moloch* is derived from the Hebrew word *mlk*, which usually translates to melek or king, it could very well be the latter. But even that's not good."

"God help us," Pax murmured and crossed himself.

"Okay," Dev said. "I'm extra glad that Lark and I took some time to put more wards and shields and protections on the estate, and that we gave you all additional weapons by allowing you to converse with those who can see this thing, even if he doesn't allow *us* to. We'll have at least one dearly departed assigned to each group so they're there if needed." He looked around at the group.

He checked his watch, and several of us did the same. "Let's do another equipment check. Make sure all the batteries are fully charged and that everybody has spares. Tonight, more than ever, let's try to stay in touch. We only have two investigating groups, so that should be a little easier. Pick someone to be your point person, and let's do a status check every hour if possible. Doesn't have to be on camera if you can't work it in. Just make it a priority."

Just as we all moved to do that, and the ghost crew disappeared again—yes, just . . . disappeared. Poof. Gone—Birdie walked into the room. I looked up when I caught the movement and took in her face. She looked a bit pale. I got up and walked to her.

"Hey," I said, catching her eye. "Are you okay?"

She met my gaze, but it seemed to take her a minute for my words to register, as if she were deep in thought. "Huh?" She shook her head. "Oh. Yeah, I'm fine. Just a bit out of sorts."

Something was going on. "Is it anything we need to be concerned with? You're with Pax, Aaron, and me tonight."

"No, no. It's just some personal stuff. I'll shove it all down and be all business in a few. Promise." She flashed me a grin, but it looked a bit forced. Nothing like her usual easy, genuine, and utterly warm smiles.

I put my hand on her shoulder. "You know you can talk to me, right?"

She pulled me in for a hug and said, "I know. Thank you." She leaned back and looked at me again, keeping her hands on my biceps. "I'm okay. Really." She winked and then walked away. I watched her head over to where Turner sat behind the monitors. I swore I heard her say something to him about a colt—a horse? the gun?—but it made no sense, so I just shrugged it off and got back to work.

* * *

AT FULL DARK, we split up into our groups and headed to our respective investigating areas. As I walked to the back of the house, following Birdie and Aaron, Pax caught up to me and grabbed my hand, tugging me to a stop. I turned to him.

He looked at Birdie and Aaron as they disappeared into the next room and then gazed back down at me. "I want to ask you to do something for me, but I think I know what your answer will be."

"I'm not staying back, Pax. It's not happening."

"That's not what I was going to ask." He looked really uncomfortable for a minute. "I would feel more comfortable if you wore one of my holy objects."

I scoffed and rolled my eyes. "Like that would do any good. Don't those things require belief, Pax?"

"I believe. They're mine." He looked at me more intensely, and I swore I could read between the lines. *You're mine.*

More snark about the whole god thing came to the tip of my tongue but I swallowed it down. He was being sincere, and I saw the concern in the features of his face. If me wearing a stupid piece of jewelry for him alleviated some of that, what harm would it do?

"Okay, fine," I huffed. "Pin me."

He laughed as I'd intended. "Did you just say, 'pin me?'"

I shrugged. "Isn't that what you old-timers used to call it when someone gave you their class ring or Letterman pin and asked you to go steady?"

"Are you saying you want to go steady with me?" he asked, a smile flirting with his gorgeous lips.

"I dunno. I'll write you a note later and ask you to check yes or no."

"You're ridiculous," he said and then reached up to his neck, unclasping something right under his Adam's apple. When he pulled his hand away, a twisted brown necklace hung from his fingers, a square of material at the back.

"What is it?" I asked, my curiosity getting the best of me.

"It's called a scapular," he said. "The Brown Scapular, to be exact. It has a longer official name, but it's not important right now. What *is* important, is that, in my faith, it's a very powerful holy object. A sign of salvation, a protection against danger and possession, and a pledge of peace. It used to be my grandfather's."

I really looked at it then. While I didn't believe in it, something about having another physical tie to Pax in what would probably be a really harrowing night felt . . . comforting. We had just found out that his grandfather was the one who'd saved me from Moon Call, and having a tie to him transferred from Pax to me felt oddly poetic in some way.

I twisted my hair into a bun as I'd meant to do before anyway, secured it, and then gave Pax a what-are-you-waiting-for gesture. He secured the necklace around my throat, the square of material to the back, and then cupped my cheek in his hand.

His baby blues captured my gaze as he ran his thumb over the apple of my cheek and then shifted so he could run it along my bottom lip. My breath caught, and my eyes closed. When I opened them again, he was looking at me so intently, I felt the heat all the way to my toes.

I rose on tiptoe and brushed my lips to his, winding my arms around his neck. He pulled me close and stole my breath entirely with the intensity of the embrace, his tongue seeking mine and his hands gripping. When he pulled back, he kissed me quickly once more and then placed kisses on my forehead, both cheeks, and then my nose before taking a deep breath.

"We'd better catch up," he said, and all I could do was nod.

When we entered the back room where I'd crawled

into the wall some weeks ago, I saw Birdie and Aaron talking quietly by the wall with the jagged opening. Lark looked over when we got closer, and Aaron started the camera rolling.

"Hey," she said to Pax and me. "This place feels worse than usual tonight. Don't let your guards down, okay?"

We both nodded, and my gaze was drawn up to the yawning maw near the ceiling. It was bigger than the last time we were here, and I wondered if Roch had widened it so that Lark could do what she needed to do with the chest that was up there. Just as I was turning away, I swore I saw a hand reach through the opening, grasp air, and then disappear back in, but I was sure it had to be nerves. I shook it off and then refocused back on Birdie and Aaron.

"Do you want me to get some readings?" I asked.

"Yes, let's start there," Birdie said, and I dropped what I liked to call my mad-scientist kit to pull out my equipment. I took air quality readings and some other metrics and reported the findings to my team and the camera. Besides some elevated and inconsistent electromagnetic frequencies, which we always saw in here, everything seemed okay. Environmentally, anyway.

Earlier, during our team meeting, we'd discussed how to handle anything that may arise tonight for the audience. They didn't know that we could see and hear spirits now, and we had to find a way to both use that and keep it status quo for the viewers. Dev told us to remember to over-explain. We tried to do that anyway to cover anybody catching a show in the middle of an investigation, but tonight we had to remember that while all of us could see certain things, the public could not.

As Pax and Birdie did an EVP session with the Wonder Box, I walked the perimeter of the room with my Handycam, and Aaron kept watch on all of us with his camera.

I turned just as Pax asked, "Who do we have here with us tonight?"

The Wonder Box squawked and then a voice came through. "Píngguǒ. *Leave now.*"

Pax and Birdie shared a look. "Seiko, is that you?" Larken asked.

"*Not safe,*" said the voice. "*Wants you.*"

All three of them looked over at me and I shrugged. "Bring it."

"Sky!" Pax admonished. "No, no, no. You can't say things like that. Provocation can only be done by the faithful—preferably a priest." He pointed at himself with annoyance and then looked around nervously.

"What?" I asked. "This thing is really pissing me off now. I'm fucking tired of it messing with my head."

Lark hurried over to me and took my free hand. "I know, Sky." She gestured to Aaron and Pax. "We all do. But there are rules. And we follow them for a reason. You *know* these rules. Dev and I taught them to you when you first joined the team. If you can't follow those rules tonight, I'm not sure we can have you here."

That just pissed me off more, but I took stock of

how I was feeling and realized it wasn't entirely like me. I was abnormally angry. And at those I knew were only trying to help me. Maybe Birdie was right. Perhaps this was a bad idea. Maybe I should just be alone for a while.

That thought hit me, too. Being alone was exactly the *wrong* idea. It was precisely what Dev had told us *not* to do.

"Ugh, Christ. What's that smell?" Aaron said and raised a hand to his nose.

It hit me as well then. Something like spoiled meat.

"We're not alone," Birdie said and looked around, her breath making the air cloud. It had dropped several degrees in an instant.

Paxton crossed himself and moved closer to me, reaching for my Handycam where I had it just hanging by my side. *What the fuck?* That was also completely unlike me because I knew that we were supposed to keep rolling at all times, no matter what happened. I shook my head and handed it over.

"Something's going on, guys. I . . . I don't feel right."

Birdie just nodded and shared a look with Pax that I couldn't quite translate.

"Maybe we should get her out of here," Pax said and pointed the Handycam at Birdie.

The Wonder Box bleeped and blarted again, and a sinister voice came through this time.

"Too late."

CHAPTER 22

~Paxton~

*J*ust as I registered what the voice on the Wonder Box had said, Sky flew through the air, looking as if she were jerked by a string through her abdomen. She didn't stop until she slammed into the wall to my left, still at least two feet off the floor, and stuck to the drywall like a bug on flypaper.

Schuyler's terrified screams ripped open something in me, and I barely registered Aaron and Birdie yelling and rushing to help her.

I couldn't move. I was frozen with shock.

Suddenly, she seemed to go limp, and everything snapped back into place and restarted. I dropped the camera and rushed forward, moving to help Sky.

Elbowing my way through Lark and Aaron, I had almost reached her when she slid up the wall and *into* it, her limp body disappearing into the opening near the ceiling.

"NOOOOO!" I screamed, looking around for a ladder to get up there. Thankfully, Roch and the crew had left more equipment when they came to widen the wall opening.

I barely heard Birdie yelling a spell, and Aaron on the walkie, radioing the other team for help as I pulled the ladder over to the opening and crawled up and in. I tugged my cell out of my pocket and clicked on the flashlight app. The LED light didn't reach far enough, but at least I could see.

"Padre!" someone yelled from down below, but I was too focused on looking around for Sky to really let it register. She had to be up here, and I had to find her. I panned the area again and thought I saw something in the far-left corner. I moved in that direction, only to stop short when a figure appeared right in front of me. At first, I thought it must be one of the mannequins that Sky had mentioned during our first trip to Lamour, but then it spoke.

"You must help her," said the woman. When I moved my cellphone light closer, I saw that some light made its way through her. She was a ghost—the same one we had seen with Lance on the video.

"Seiko?" I asked.

She nodded and pointed, and I followed the line of her finger. There, on the dirt-strewn floor was my scapular. My stomach plummeted, and an ice-water rush of adrenaline-laced fear froze my veins. I bent and picked it up, noticing that the clasp was broken. I put it in my pocket and turned back to Seiko.

"Help—" She pointed, but before she could finish the sentence, another figure appeared. This one tall and thin in a robe. The same one we'd seen on the video. Lance. He sneered at me and then jerked Seiko back against him, both of them disappearing almost instantly.

I shone my light in the direction she had started to point when I heard noises behind me. I turned, ready to defend myself, when Dev and Larken came up behind me.

"Where is she?" Dev asked, his headlamp nearly blinding me.

I couldn't find the words. Could only shake my head. I was terrified. She didn't have protection and we had no idea what this thing would do to her.

"I feel her," Birdie said, and I looked over at her. She had her eyes closed and a focused expression on her face, her flashlight hanging by her side. She batted her lashes open and pointed to the right.

We all ran over there and looked around frantically. Finally, I saw something, a flash of white that I thought might be her WHO LEFT THE BAG OF IDIOTS OPEN? shirt. I moved in that direction and stopped short in my tracks. There was indeed a body there, but it wasn't Sky's. Bones gleamed in the low light, playing peek-a-boo with us through the dirt on the floor. Clearly, nobody from the construction crew had made it up this far, or we probably wouldn't have gotten the opportunity to investigate the place. It would have been a crime scene. Seemed we'd found where the coven stashed their bodies.

I carefully moved around the remains, as did Dev and Birdie, and headed farther back, closer to the corner. My light snagged on a shape, and I exhaled when I saw the white tee I had been looking for earlier. Her favorite leather jacket hung off one shoulder, and she was still slumped, but if Birdie had felt her earlier, that meant she was alive. I wouldn't say okay, but she was alive.

I moved to her as fast as I could and crouched down, carefully feeling for a pulse. It was strong, and her breathing, while a little shallow and uneven, was steady. I looked at Larken.

"Can you tell if she has any injuries? Can I move her?" I asked.

Birdie closed her eyes and concentrated again. When she looked at me once more, she appeared solemn but hopeful. "I don't think so," she said. "I don't sense any acute injuries. But she's clearly unconscious, and there's . . . there's something else. I don't know exactly what." She looked at Dev.

"Yeah, I sense it, too." He reached into his pocket and pulled out a gris-gris bag, murmuring over it and blowing on it before handing it to me. "Put this some-where on her person. I have a feeling we're going to need it."

I took it from him and did as he suggested, slipping it into the front pocket of her jeans. I picked her up as carefully as I could, cradling her against me. Dev and Birdie led me to the opening and then told me to sit and wait with Sky as they got out and figured out a way to get her down safely.

Sooner than I had anticipated later, they called up and told me to bring her to the edge. When I maneuvered us over there, I saw that they were all positioned just under the opening on a long table, arms staggered and outstretched to accept her from me and gently lower her down. We got her out, and they pulled the makeshift gurney out of the way, repositioning the ladder so I could make my way down and over to the table.

"Sky, can you hear me?" I said, gently touching her face. Nothing. No reaction at all.

"Uh, Dev," Dakota said, speaking up for the first time. I looked up and saw him turn to her, then we both looked in the direction she pointed. There was a huge floor-to-ceiling window across from us, and each of us was depicted in the reflection of the dark glass. What showed there that we didn't see with our own eyes, was the undulating, miasmic shadow that rose from Sky's body, covering her from head to toe.

"*Merde*," Dev said, and nearly everyone echoed him with a curse of their choice.

I looked back down at Sky and wondered how to help her. This thing had its claws in her and I didn't think I was strong enough to get rid of it. I didn't even know if Dev, Birdie, and me working together would be able to vanquish it. A sense of failure started to swamp me, but I batted it away. That was what the malevolence wanted. It wanted to break me down. Make me feel inadequate. It wanted me to give up and let it have her.

I wouldn't let that happen.

I needed to remain calm and keep my composure, even if I wanted to absolutely lose it right now.

"Can someone bring me my bag? It's near the door." I was afraid to take my eyes off Sky, but I needed my gear. Hanlen hurried up next to me and set the bag near me on a clear bit of the table. I undid the clips and flipped up the top, rummaging inside for my crucifix, holy water, Bible, and exorcism rite literature. I placed all the items on the table and then dumped the bag to the floor, making room.

"Are you prepared for this?" Dev asked, and I looked up to meet his turquoise eyes.

"Honestly? I don't know. And I'm trying really hard not to lose my shit right now." I shook my head. "I'm not sure I can tackle something this big alone."

Just as I said that, Sky started to stir and opened her eyes. Only it wasn't her soulful brown eyes we saw. Her pupils were so big, it looked as if the black were bleeding into the sclera, and her lips were twisted into a snarl I couldn't ever imagine her perfect mouth making.

"That's not Sky," Birdie said and started mumbling

an incantation under her breath. I heard Dev join in, speaking in a language I didn't understand.

"You four." I pointed to the closest team members. "I need help holding her down. Secure her to the table. Don't hurt her, but don't let her move around too much either. The rest of you, hold hands. If you can't join in with Dev or Lark, say the Lord's Prayer—even if you don't believe. If you don't know it, listen to the person next to you saying it and just tap into that energy. Do it. Do it now." They all did as I said, the murmurs becoming a background buzz that helped me to focus. I was just happy that I'd at least had the presence of mind to do that.

When I looked back at Sky, she snapped and snarled, the evil entity clearly making its presence known. Then, just as suddenly, her eyes cleared, and she looked around, seeming confused.

"Pax? What's going on?" she asked, and James moved to let her go.

"No!" I yelled, looking the younger man in the eye. "There are several stages to possession. Presence— which we just saw. The evil entity making itself known. Pretense—which we're seeing now, where they pretend to be back to normal, and then there are a few others before expulsion. Since it hasn't gotten its hooks in too deep yet, we may be able to bypass some of those middle ones. But this still isn't Sky. And don't let it fool you into thinking it is. I want to believe it, too, but we can't. Not now. Not yet."

"O—okay," he said and resumed his hold.

"Clever priest," Sky growled in a voice that wasn't at all hers. "Mmm," she said, undulating a little on the table. "Do you know that it isn't her since you spent so much time in her sweet, sweet body lately?"

I tried not to let it bother me. It wanted a reaction, and I didn't want to give it one.

"Too bad you lost your collar, little priest," the non-Sky taunted. "You may have defeated my minion back then, took back the tasty morsel that should have been mine and saved that child, but you won't take this one. You won't steal from me twice, *Padre*. Your little girl-friend should have become a part of me three decades ago. I will have my due!"

She surged up on the table, fighting the hold the others had on her.

"Jesus Christ, she's strong," Aaron said, the muscles in his huge arms bunching with the effort to keep her down.

I opened my bottle of holy water and sprinkled some over her. Invoking the Holy Trinity. She hissed and thrashed. I held my crucifix against her shirt between her breasts, and she screamed, yelling that it burned.

"Keep up with the prayers and spells. Don't stop," I instructed, my gut a roiling mess.

I flipped open the Bible and started reading. I read from Ephesians. I read from Peter. I read from Leviticus—I only pissed it off. I'd seen no marked improvement, and I and the rest of the team were sweaty messes of exhaustion.

"I can't do this," I said and couldn't stop the tears if I wanted to. "I can't save her."

"You can." I heard a voice and looked up to see Burke standing in front of me.

"How?" I begged, my body shaking with fear and my voice trembling.

"Reagan and the rest of our crew have Seiko and Lance occupied. They're trying to get Seiko away from the bastard and make sure he can't do anything to thwart what you guys are doing. All you have to worry about right now is this." He pointed at Sky on the table.

"But I can't do this. I'm not strong enough. I don't have enough experience. I need help. And I can't get my dad to help because he won't lift a finger until the archdiocese says he can. And we know how long it takes for the Church to approve an exorcism. *If* they approve one at all."

"You don't need your dad," Burke said, and I got even more confused.

I glanced back at Sky and saw that she had calmed a bit, but she was panting now, and growls issued from her slightly parted lips that I knew weren't hers. "If not him, then who?" I looked back up and almost fell on my ass. Burke wasn't there anymore. Instead, I saw a face that used to bring me so much joy. I saw a face I missed like a limb some days.

"Grandda?"

CHAPTER 23

~Paxton~

"Hello, my son," Grandda said and moved closer. He looked the same as I remembered him. Same ice-blue eyes as mine. Full, thick head of snow-white hair. No stooped posture for him—he always carried himself with a regality I envied. He wore his uniform of black pants, black shirt, and bright white priest's collar.

"I can help you, Paxton," he said, and I became even more confused. Then it hit me. This may not be my grandfather. Demons were master manipulators and liars. They could cause all sorts of hallucinations and mess with your head to get what they wanted.

"Be gone, evil one," I said and brandished my crucifix at the specter.

"That's really Dougal, Padre," Dev said, and I looked over at him.

"How can you be sure?" I asked.

"It's part of my gifts. I always know a spirit from an illusion." He resumed his chanting, and I looked back at the ghost, realizing that I wouldn't feel such a connection if it weren't Grandda.

"I've missed you so much," I said.

"And I, you, my boy," he said with a sad smile and then looked at Sky. She'd started writhing in earnest again, and the team was having trouble keeping her down with as exhausted as they had to be, and how strong the demon likely was. "If you want my help, all you need do is ask. We can help each other to right a wrong. To vanquish an evil that has no place on this plane. I thought I saved her once. Let me help you ensure she's safe now."

"How?" I asked.

"Do you still have the scapular I left to you?" he asked.

I pulled it out of my pocket and held it up. "I gave it to Sky, but the demon ripped it off when it hauled her into the storage space. The clasp's broken."

"It doesn't matter. We just need a tether."

"A . . . tether?" I asked.

"If you allow it," Grandda said, "I can enter your body temporarily via the tether that ties us. We have both blood and an earthly object. Once I do, you will be yourself, but you will be imbued with all my knowledge and skills. You will have the blessing of the

Church because *I* have the blessing of the Church and I didn't lose that. Even in death."

"You can . . . we can do that?"

"We can."

"Yes. Yes, of course, I give you permission. *Please* help me save her."

He moved closer to me, near the hand that still held the scapular. I felt a tingling sensation all over my body, little bolts of electricity, and the air felt a tiny bit colder. He reached out and touched me, and my body jerked. It was . . . strange. It didn't hurt, it just felt weird. In a couple of breaths, things regulated, and he was right—I knew everything I needed to know to kick this demon's ass.

I squatted and reached into my messenger bag. I didn't usually wear a stole because I didn't exactly have the right to do so anymore, but these weren't normal circumstances. I dug out my purple stole and draped it over my neck, looping my rosary over my head to join my cross and Saint Michael medallion. When I stood again, I handed one exorcism rite book off to Hanlen and opened the other, swallowing the lump in my throat.

"Page one eighty-six," I told Hanlen. "Only read the responses, and only when I tell you. Everyone else,"—I looked around at the others—"echo what she says when she says it."

I sprinkled Sky with holy water again and once again held my crucifix against her chest, trying not to let her thrashing and straining into shapes that shouldn't be humanly possible derail me. I started the rite, invoking the Archangel in the name of the Father, Son, and Holy Spirit. I repeated the holy water and kept going, giving blessings, thanking those who would be helping, and asking for assistance. When I reached the participation portion of the rite, I signaled for Hanlen to answer after I read my parts, and everyone else echoed her. The entire time, Sky thrashed and roared, spoke in tongues, and spat vile lies.

At one point, she turned her head to Larken and told her that she could no longer run. Could no longer hide from her past and those who would find and destroy her. I saw Birdie's face pale, but she was a strong witch and a professional and she maintained her composure and kept up with her spell. I had no time to think on that, but I would ask her about it when this was all said and done.

Because it *would* be done.

"Be gone, unclean spirit. We drive you from this innocent. All satanic powers, infernal invaders, wicked legions, assemblies, and sects, we command you to leave. The Most High compels you. The power of God compels you. Jesus Christ, our Savior, compels you. The Holy Mother compels you."

Her back bowed, and I heard a crack, my heart falling to my stomach. I felt myself start to waver a little, but I had to keep it together.

I yanked my rosary off and wrapped it around my fist, putting my hand on Sky's head. It kicked up her fighting a bit, but everyone seemed to be holding well.

"Be gone, Moloch, devourer of souls. Stoop beneath the powerful hand of God, tremble in his name and flee this place."

Sky roared, the demon not liking that we knew its name. "I will roast you on a spit and eat you like I should have crunched on this one's fragile bones."

"No, you will not!" I shouted. "Sky, I know you're in there. Fight. Come back to us!"

I sprinkled her with holy water again and winced at the hiss, even though I knew it was the demon and not her. "Be gone, Moloch, destroyer of children. Tremble in the presence of the light of Heaven and return to Hell where you belong. The power of Christ compels you. I command you by the power invested in me, by this joining of blood, by the one who defeated you before . . . LEAVE this vessel!!" I shouted the last and pressed my hand a little harder against Sky's forehead. Her back bowed, and she shrieked, letting loose a sound unlike anything I'd heard from a human before. It nearly tore a hole in my heart.

Suddenly, a sickening black mass poured out of her mouth in a cloud the size of a basketball and then exploded, sending all of us flying back.

And then . . . nothing.

* * *

WHEN I WOKE, my head aching and my throat raw, I sat up gingerly, looking around and noticing that everyone else was doing the same. Some helped others. Some simply sat there with heads in hands. I looked up at the table and saw Sky still lying there, her body prone.

I flew up and ran over, relief flooding me as I saw her chest rise and fall with breath. Her color was better, but I didn't dare trust that everything was okay. Not until she opened her eyes, and I knew for sure. There was one big difference, though. A thick chunk of her hair had turned a bright, snowy white. I fingered the tendril, hoping it was the worst of the fallout from what'd happened.

Just as I was thinking that, I noticed movement out of the corner of my eye. I looked over to find my grandfather.

"We did it, son," he said. "Moloch is gone. Back to Hell where he should have been all those years ago."

I looked back down at Sky and brushed some more hair away from her face. "Are you sure?" I asked.

"I'm sure," he answered.

I looked over at him. "Thank you."

"No need. This was my purpose. It's why I'm still here. Now, I can finally rest."

I hadn't even thought of that. This unfinished business was why he hadn't been able to move on to paradise. Decades of lingering. "I'm so sorry, Grandda."

"It's not your fault, Paxton." He smiled. "And God's plan is great. He just sometimes plays the long game."

It was my turn to smile. "I've missed you so much. What happened when you disappeared?"

He shrugged. "I didn't disappear, I just went away. After everything that happened with the Moon Call

Coven, I was never really myself again. I hid it well from you and your sister when I was allowed to see you—by the grace of God alone. You were going through a lot on your own, and your father didn't want anything to do with either of us. So, I bought a little secluded place in the mountains in Montana. I was oppressed and virtually hunted by the public, and it was better and safer for you all if I wasn't around. If we were in olden times, they probably would have come after me with pitchforks in the night." He shook his head.

"But what happened? Did the oppression become possession and finally kill you?"

He laughed ruefully. "Not at all. Bad tires and a snow-slick road did me in."

"So, it really was just an accident?"

He nodded. "It's been so wonderful seeing you, Paxton. I'm so very proud of you. Never let anyone, even your father, tell you that what you did was wrong. You saved that child's life. He would have died had you not intervened. And if you had waited for the Vatican to give you permission, it may have been too late. I'm sorry that it cost you so much, but . . ." He looked down at Sky, and a smile stretched his face. "Then again, seems God had other plans." He looked back up at me. "Do you love her?"

I took a deep breath, whispering so only he could hear me. "I think I do. I think I've been falling for years without realizing it. Almost losing her during this investigation just made me face it. But she's nowhere near ready to hear that, and I'm not entirely sure I'm ready to tell her. But, yeah, I think I do." I nodded.

"I wish I could hug you. I'll just have to settle for saying congratulations. When the time is right, you'll tell her. And you'll see what she has to say about that."

I smiled.

Dev walked up to me and addressed Grandda. "Father."

"Hello, Deveraux."

"Thank you for everything you did to help."

Grandda inclined his head. "Of course."

"Is there anything we can do for you? Do you need me to reach out to Papa Legba to ferry you home?"

"Not necessary, my child. But thank you for the offer. I think my ride just arrived." As he said that, a bright light appeared from all around us. It was so brilliant, so beautiful, it was hard to look away, even though it was so searing. The fear of blindness was real.

A disembodied, *"God be with you,"* surrounded us, and then the light disappeared, along with my grandfather.

"And also with you," I whispered, looking down at Sky, just as she opened her eyes.

"Pax?" she breathed, looking confused.

"I'm here, Sky."

"What the actual fuck just happened?"

I laughed. This would be a very interesting story to tell.

CHAPTER 24

~Schuyler~

t had been a couple of weeks since the events at the Lamour Mansion, and I was finally starting to feel like myself again. I still had a hard time swallowing what Pax and the team had told me had happened, but I couldn't refute the proof. Our cameras and microphones had caught everything, and I'd watched it all back, feeling as if I were viewing one of the horror movies I loved so much, not my real life.

It helped a little that we had been able to debunk *some* of the things that had gone on outside of that. The front door window shattering had a logical explanation —there was an oak tree in the side yard, and there had been a storm that day—we'd gotten the results of the samples I'd sent in, and there was indeed some mold in the home, and the estate had some ground wire issues, which could definitely explain some of the high electromagnetic frequency readings. Not to mention, Dev did uncover that two ley lines intersected under the property. Knowing all that—even though I didn't know much about ley lines—settled a small piece of my mind. The one that wanted to hold tight to absolutes and not get sucked into the things that defied explanation.

I'd also been doing some video sessions with Harper to work through some stuff, and it was really helping. We'd discussed everything that had been uncovered about my past and talked about how to deal with it moving forward with my parents and just my life in general. We'd even unpacked a bit of the coincidence of me getting a tattoo that tied back to my original name. I'd just felt really drawn to the design and couldn't shake it until I saved up enough money to get it. Mom *did* tell me recently that the blanket I'd been wrapped in when Pax's grandfather delivered me to them had had an apple tree embroidered in the corner. I vaguely remembered using it for my dolls as a kid. Maybe that's where the subliminal suggestion had come from. Who knew?

As for the show, the network had gone crazy for the episode after everything had been edited and gave us all raises and a promise for another extension. *The Lamour Affliction* went live last night and got the highest ratings we'd ever had. I couldn't bring myself to watch it. Living through it was enough. Reviewing it after the team caught me up on what'd happened was more than enough. Seeing it all again, even with careful editing and creative license—and Hanlen said that Van and Lennie did some spectacular things to make it all flow smoothly since for most of it we were in the fight of our lives and not actively investigating—well, that was beyond what my mind could handle.

I'd actually asked Dev if I could take a little sabbatical. I needed to think over everything that'd happened in my life, how things had changed, and come to terms with it all. He'd easily agreed, and so, here I was, on vacation for the first time in forever. Actually, the entire team was taking a break. Not too much, as we had a huge compound in the Ninth Ward to investigate, but we were all due some R&R after so many back-to-back-to-back filmings, and such a long stretch without any time off—not to mention everything that had happened with the team. Deaths. A kidnapping. Murder. Betrayal. Turnover. We all needed some personal time to process. It would be good for everyone and *Haunted New Orleans* for us to reset.

From my cozy spot on the porch, I looked around at the wilderness around me—the still lake glistening like a jewel in the barely risen sun, the lush trees surrounding the area like a gorgeous, natural fence, and the majestic mountains in the distance standing like silent sentinels with watchful eyes. It was breathtaking. I'd never considered myself a nature-y kind of girl—until I was in it. Now, I wasn't sure I wanted to leave. I should probably be concerned at yet another change to my personality, but cut a girl a break. A lot of shit had happened. At least I wasn't still oppressed and acting like a lunatic.

A mug dropped down in front of my face, and I gratefully accepted it with a smile, turning my head to take in the bearer of the mana. Yes, I was getting used to drinking my coffee hot. Stranger things had happened.

"Good morning," Pax said, leaning down to give me a thorough kiss and swiping his fingers down the now-bright-pink streak I had in my jet-black hair, tucking it behind an ear and making me shiver. I'd finally gotten the fashion color pop I'd always wanted. It'd only taken me being possessed and almost dying to turn it white enough that I could.

I glanced over at Paxton next to me, watching him take a sip of his black brew. Damn the man was hot. I'd never tire of thinking it. And he'd literally put his life—and if you asked him, his *soul*—on the line for me. What more could a girl ask for?

"It is a good morning, isn't it?" I said, looking back out at the scene before us. "I'm really glad you had Hanlen dig into your grandfather's estate. This gorgeous place was just sitting here going to waste." I looked back at Pax. "I can't believe your dad didn't tell you that Dougal left you this."

"Honestly, I'm not surprised by anything my father does or doesn't do anymore. I'm sure it was a manipulation ploy that he planned to use later for God only knows what reason. I'm just glad that it's all settled now and it's getting the love it deserves."

"So am I. I want to come here often so you can give me what *I* deserve," I said with a waggle of my brows.

He smiled. "We can come here as much as you want. What's mine is yours."

"Well, considering I had my hands and tongue all over it last night, I hope so. I mean . . . I licked it. Pretty sure that means I can keep it." I winked.

We sat in companiable silence for a while, just breathing in the crisp mountain air.

"What are you going to do about Lamour?" he asked, turning to me.

My stomach dropped a little. Apparently, given everything that had been going on for so long with the mansion, the current owners finally gave up the ghost. Roch called a meeting about four days after our final interview with him to go over the investigation data and told us that the owners had let his entire crew go and gave the property back to the bank.

Given everything that'd come to light during the investigation, representatives for the bank had hired Roch back to finish the job—after the police did what they had to do with the bodies in the storage area, anyway—and then did some digging as due diligence. As it turned out, as Lance's only surviving child, *I* was the rightful owner of Lamour.

Apparently, Lance's father's will had a provision stating that the estate should be passed down in the family until no other family members remained. But it got better. There was even a boatload of money set aside in trust for its upkeep and maintenance. And all of that had been uncovered when additional research was done.

So . . . that big, beautiful home, the one that had been both a dream and a nightmare for me, was mine. And I still didn't know what to do with it. Luckily, I didn't have to decide immediately. I'd told the lawyers that I needed some time to think things over but would let them know how I wanted to proceed before the end of the year.

The other kicker? The one that may end up making a difference in the long run . . . Apparently, my biological mom was still there.

Dev and Birdie had helped nearly all of the spirits cross over, but Seiko didn't want to go. She'd said that she had spent too many years living on this plane and didn't know where she'd end up if she crossed over. At least on Earth, she knew what to expect. And now that Lance was gone—Burke had told us that he'd decided to follow Moloch, wherever the evil bastard went— Seiko was free to live . . . or, at least, *exist* in peace.

Part of me was happy for her. She had practically been born into a world of evil. And she had done the right thing by trying to save me—both during the investigation *and* when I was just a child. As it turned out, *Seiko* was the one who'd asked Shelly/Michelle to turn the coven in, even knowing that it would mean her downfall—potentially both of theirs.

The other part of me didn't know how I felt about her being there if *I* was there. She was still tied to the house as her home base, even if she could roam. And even though I could no longer see her, when I compartmentalized everything I'd gone through, I knew I'd be back on the science-weighted side of things. It was just who I was. I knew I couldn't explain away anything that'd happened and had to accept that it was real. *Somehow.* But it was still something my subconscious fought against, and I figured it always would. Before I took up residence in the place—if I did —I needed to make peace with the fact that Mommy Dearest would be there more often than not.

"Earth to Sky." Pax interrupted my thoughts.

"Yes, that's my mom's store's name. Is this supposed to be one of those brain teasers for *mature* adults? Reminding yourself of things you already know?" He rolled his eyes as I'd intended, and I just quirked my lip.

I looked at him before answering his earlier question. "I'm still not sure what I'm going to do," I said honestly. "On the one hand, why wouldn't I want to live there? It's stunning, and it's paid for. But on the other hand . . ."

"You were almost killed there."

"Yeah, there is that." My mouth went dry, and I took a drink of my coffee. He knew just how to make it for me with the perfect ratio of cream and sugar. He knew how to do *so* many things perfectly. I smiled inwardly.

Things with Lamour had been a shitshow, but I didn't regret a single moment spent with Paxton. I tipped back my head and closed my eyes, just enjoying the moment.

"Sky?"

"Mm-hmm."

"Can I tell you something?"

"Sure."

He cleared his throat. "You know that you—"

"Have a great ass?"

"Well, yeah, you do. But that's not what I was going to say."

I grinned and rocked my head back and forth on the chair back. "What were you going to say?"

"I was going to say that—"

"The answer to everything is forty-two?"

He laughed. "Well, I'm not saying it's not. Mr. Adams would definitely agree with you, but that's not what I was going to say, either. I was going to say that I think I—"

My eyes flew open, and I looked at him. "Stop right there."

"What? What'd I say?" he asked, a look of shock on his handsome face.

"Nothing. *Yet.*"

"O-o-o-kay."

I sighed. "Here's the thing, Pax. This is good. We're good. Everything's really fucking good right now. I'm just not ready to hear what I think you were about to say yet."

He nodded. "Okay. But for the record, I think things are good, too."

"Well, *good.*" I smiled. "The thing is, I don't need labels to be happy. I don't need to prove anything to anybody but you. And vice versa. And you did that by saving my ass back at Lamour, and in all the little things you've done since. And, frankly, it's nobody else's business. Why do they get to decide what love and marriage and happiness looks like for us?"

"They don't."

"So, you *do* get it?" I asked, looking at him, staring straight into his gorgeous, glacial-blue eyes. Eyes that never failed to take my breath. There was so much depth in those beautiful baby blues. So much . . . *goodness.*

"I get it. I just . . ." He sighed. "I told you when we first slept together that I like labels. And in my mind, Sky, I'm yours."

That made something inside me warm, and I smiled. "You know what? I'm actually okay with that," I said, and the corner of my mouth kicked up.

"Well, hallelujah." He brought my hand to his lips and kissed the back of it.

I felt as if I needed to say more. Just to make sure he understood. "I can see a future for us, Pax. I don't know exactly what that looks like, but I *can* picture it. And I like what I see. I want to live in the moment. I want to savor each passing second of every single day and bask in whatever life throws at us."

"Can we do that together?" he asked, the look on his face so pleading, my heart twisted. He didn't need to say the words—those three that were said so much and with such flippancy that they sometimes started not to mean anything anymore. I knew exactly how he felt just by looking at him. And it made me happier than I ever expected to feel.

"I did say 'us,' didn't I?"

"Fair point. So, if I someday ask you again if I can tell you something?"

"I may let you. That day. I may not. I dunno. We'll have to see." I winked.

"You're mean." He stood, picked me up out of my chair, and plopped back down in his with me in his lap. "What if I decide I want to ask you a question someday in the future?"

"You can ask me all sorts of questions, Pax. Doesn't mean I'll answer them. Especially not the way you want me to. I mean, you know I can be contrary." I shrugged, teasing. "But as for *that* one, meh . . . you can ask, I suppose. Just know that I'm not stepping foot in a church, and there will be no white involved. But seeing you in a tux . . . mmm, oh, yeah,"—I wiggled in his lap— "that might be worth saying yes for."

"Duly noted. And I'd suffer that. But only for you," he said and laughed before kissing my neck.

And he didn't stop there. He licked and nibbled, tugged and caressed. He worked me into a frenzy right there on the porch, and just as I was about to crest that hill and fall into oblivion from his hands alone—still completely clothed, I might add—he . . . freaking stopped.

"Goddamnit, Pax. Are you fucking serious right now?"

"He *still* has nothing to do with this."

"You're damn right, he doesn't," I growled. "You'd better finish what you started there or—" I squealed as he stood and threw me over his shoulder, taking me into the cabin.

He bounced me onto the bed and then stripped us both completely, getting back to what he'd started outside and making me see stars not once but twice. By the time he finally joined with me, I was crazy with lust —and yeah, maybe a little bit of love . . . but he didn't need to know that. *Yet*. When he moved in that perfect way he did, knowing exactly what I liked, intuiting precisely what I needed in the moment, I cried out.

When we both came down from our epic highs, he cuddled me close, and I basked in the comfort and safety I felt in his arms.

"This. Right here. *This* is where I want to be."

He kissed my head. "I'm not going anywhere, Sky. We'll take each day as it comes and live them all to their fullest. We'll enjoy each other and our friends and our jobs and make every day mean something." He squeezed me tight. "With no labels." He paused. "At least, not yet."

"I dunno. I have one I might want to use now?" I turned over my shoulder to look at him.

He quirked a brow. "What's that?"

"Can I call you daddy?"

He burst out laughing and rolled us. "Why don't we just stick with Padre?"

I pouted, shoving out my bottom lip and giving him big, puppy-dog eyes.

He pinned my hands over my head, looking down at me, a flurry of emotions in his gaze. "Oh, I'll make you call me daddy, all right." He kissed me then. Long, languidly, and deep. I almost came from that alone.

"Mmm." I purred. "Bless me, Father, for I have sinned."

"I'm sure I can come up with some good penance. Why don't we start now?"

"What are you waiting for?"

THE END

BONUS CONTENT

Do you want more?

How about a sneak peek into how everything with *Malum Discordiae* started?

Check out the short story below from Seiko Chen's point of view, taking place on that fateful night in October. I wrote it for a Halloween blog hop to give readers a small glimpse into the backstory that led to *Malum Discordiae*'s current events and shared it with my newsletter subscribers. Now, it's yours to enjoy, as well . . .

Sub Luna

Seiko watched from the shadows, her coven encircling the altar, readying for the evening's events, their black cloaks billowing like smoke in the breeze from the ceiling fan. She'd been struggling with her role in all of this. Her duty to her magical family warring with her responsibility to those of blood. She knew their dark patron demanded his due. And it had come time for her to pay. Each of her coven sisters had offered up what was asked of them. She was the last to pay tribute. She knew this was right. So why, then, did she feel so . . . *sad* all of a sudden? The grand picture, the perfect plan, was in motion. Her sacrifice would be the final cog in the machine. The fuel to feed the fire of their devotion and ensure the blessings they were to be given. And once blessed, the world—and everything beyond—would be their oyster.

She had been a part of the Moon Call Coven for her entire life. Her mother having joined when she emigrated to the States, giving birth to Seiko and bringing her up in the coven's ways. Reinforcing the family's beliefs. When her mom died, and a new priest assumed the mantle, Seiko never thought twice about staying and carrying on the family legacy. She'd seen the gifts bestowed upon the devout. Felt the power their patron blessed them with. She wanted that for herself and for her coven—always. Even if that meant giving up something that she was told not to become too attached to when instructed to become the vessel for change.

"Daughter." Seiko turned as Lance moved toward her, his stole a shocking blood-red stain against the blackness of his cloak, his hood covering most of his facial features.

Seiko clasped her hands and bowed, showing the

man the respect he was due as their high priest. "My lord."

Lance put a finger under her chin and tipped her head so her gaze reached his. "Are you ready for tonight?" he asked, running his thumb over her bottom lip before moving back a step to better look at her.

"I am, my priest. It is my time. And I am honored to be of service to our patron and the coven." She glanced in the opposite direction, looking at the tiny cradle in the corner of the room, the bundle inside quiet in sleep.

"You honor us. Brightest blessings upon you, Seiko." He leaned in and kissed her gently, something he did with nearly all his witches. Usually, she felt special, even though she knew she wasn't the only one. Tonight, she felt something else. Something she couldn't quite name. Something she didn't *want* to put a title on.

"Have you prepared?" Lance asked, and Seiko once again looked at the cradle before turning her attention back to the man in front of her.

"Not yet. I wanted to be sure my sisters didn't need anything before I left to do just that."

Lance caressed her cheek. "We are fine, my sweet. Go. Take care of your rituals. You are the guest of honor tonight, after all." He smiled, and she saw the flash of white from within the dark pit of his cowl.

She wasn't the guest of honor, but Seiko didn't say that. It wouldn't do to show her trepidation—or any kind of emotion, really. Things didn't end well for those who disagreed with Lance.

"As you wish, my lord." She bowed again and stepped back before pivoting, pulling her hood over her head to hide her face and the tears she felt prickling at the backs of her eyes. When she reached the corner, she saw that her baby was awake, staring in wonder at the world around her as if she could learn how it worked just by being in it. Such a smart, beautiful child. A pang tore through Seiko's chest, her heart feeling for a moment as if it might shatter into a million pieces. She caressed her daughter's cheek with the back of a shaking finger, feeling love flare for a moment, only for resignation to quickly replace it.

This was her duty to her coven. Her tithe to their dark lord. Her willing sacrifice tonight—her child's life offered up as a blessing on the night of the harvest moon—would be the final piece to ensure long life and everything her priest and sisters desired. She would be elevated in the coven to sit at the right hand of their leader, a direct conduit to the dark entity they served.

She swiped at her tears and straightened her spine. Tonight was not a night for sadness. Instead, it was a time for celebration. This was an *honor*.

And it wasn't as if she wouldn't see her child again.

Once she passed beyond the veil, they would be together forever. First in the realm of mist and shadows, and then on Earth once again as they were reborn. And Seiko would find a way to ensure that her darling daughter served as Moloch's mistress and was taken care of, as was her right.

After all, that is what Seiko had been promised.

However, as she gazed lovingly at her daughter's dark eyes, that knowledge didn't stop her heart from nearly beating out of her chest now, or her mind from racing, trying to think up ways that she could accomplish what was needed for the coven yet save her baby.

Unfortunately, she couldn't think of anything. Maybe after her ritual salt bath and dressing for the rite, she would have a better handle on herself and be able to think clearer.

Maybe she could talk to Lance, and he would see that this wasn't the only way to reach their goals. Maybe he would want to save his daughter as much as Seiko wanted to save her.

Or perhaps some unknown angel would take the choice out of her hands.

One never knew in a world of magic.

Haunted New Orleans Series

Eternal Spark: A Haunted New Orleans Prequel – FREE on all retailers
Memento Mori: A Haunted New Orleans Novel
Malum Discordiae: A Haunted New Orleans Novel
Mea Culpa: A Haunted New Orleans Novel – Coming Soon

Mea Culpa

COMING FALL 2022

It's easier to forgive someone at fault than to forget.

Larken Maynard knows fear. Though not the kind she's experienced while working as a paranormal investigator on *Haunted New Orleans*. Her terror stems from the sadistic, manipulative group who held her hostage for most of her life. Those who condemned her for her natural-born gifts. The people she barely escaped with her life. And now, they're back. Looking to return her to the fold and control her once again. But Lark won't go down without a fight. And the man who used to be her friend and confidant is in for a rude awakening if he thinks she will.

Kholt Leroy has never known anything but Balance of Light. They are his family, his friends; the compound his entire world. He always wondered why Larken disappeared. He'd missed her greatly. So, when asked to go and bring her home, he jumps at the chance. Unfortunately, he's unprepared for what he finds. She's not the person he remembers, and the stories she tells flips his entire world on its axis. Now, he must decide between the woman he has always cared about and the only family he's ever known.

For more information about the Haunted New Orleans Series, please click here:
https://www.ladybosspress.com/rayvnsalvador

ACKNOWLEDGMENTS

To my other half, who consistently listened to me complain about how I didn't have enough words on the page yet cheered me on even when I was working full days without interacting with him . . . thank you. And I love you. Always.

A huge shoutout to my incredible publishing team who made me feel like a *"real author"* with *Memento Mori* and cheered me on for this one, too. You guys are rock stars!

To my incredible editor, Laura, she who never complains when I repeatedly text her, wondering if I can actually meet a deadline and tells me I've got this. And my invaluable betas—Erika, Michelle, and Katrina . . . thank you so very much! I love you guys bunches.

And last—but most certainly not least—you. Yes, *you*! Thank you for getting lost in New Orleans with me. For braving the dark side alongside me. For leaving encouraging reviews and sharing about my books far and wide. For sending me notes of wonder and praise. For stopping in to hang out with me in online live chats. By reading the words between these pages, you are literally making my dreams come true. You are the absolute best!

ALSO AVAILABLE FROM RAYVN SALVADOR

The Willow Falls series:

Your Move

Seasons Change

The Fourth and Goal Series:

Blue Forty-Two

Blind Side

The Haunted New Orleans Series:

Eternal Spark – a free Haunted New Orleans short story

Memento Mori

Malum Discordiae

Coming soon . . .

Mea Culpa

PRAISE FOR RAYVN SALVADOR

"Gripping, sensual, and captivating. I was hooked from the first page of this compelling love story."

~*NY Times* bestselling author Donna Grant

"Ghosts, mysteries, romance, New Orleans, and a serial killer—Memento Mori is a perfect read!"

~*USA Today* Bestselling Author Angela Roquet

"Rayvn Salvador pens an exhilarating and romantic tale you don't want to miss!"

~*USA Today* Bestselling Author Jen Talty

"An exciting author!"

~*USA Today* Bestselling Author Michele Hauf

"Words that bring vivid imagery, along with swoon-worthy feels."

~*USA Today* Bestselling Author Tigris Eden/J.K. Rivers

"[Haunted New Orleans] is a beautiful gumbo of romance, mystery, magic, ghosts, voodoo, and love beyond the grave."
~5-Star Reviewer

"First of all, it seems like this amazing author is a descriptive genius since I truly felt like I was in New Orleans, and the paranormal aspect of it really gave me goosebumps at the end of the day, so it's safe to say that I didn't just read it, I experienced every moment."
~5-Star Reviewer

"Rayvn is a great storyteller!"
~5-Star Reviewer

ABOUT RAYVN SALVADOR

Rayvn Salvador is a lifelong bibliophile who left her eighteen-year IT career in Software Quality Assurance to live her dream: getting paid to read as a full-time editor (done as her alter ego), and to write when the mood strikes. She lives in Florida with three crazy cats and her incredibly supportive beau, dreaming about the Midwest's changing leaves as she perfects her yoga poses on the beach.

Website: Rayvnsalvador.com

facebook.com/RayvnSalvador
instagram.com/rayvnsalvador
bookbub.com/profile/rayvn-salvador